Lost Chance

Ryndy Drews had lived her entire life in the shadows of her three older sisters—Virginia, who had never had anything but A's in any subject; Vicky, the family beauty; and Valerie, charming and vivacious, voted most popular girl in school.

They had all graduated, and now Ryndy's senior year was coming. But she had yet to leave her own mark on Florida's Coral Cove High.

This would have to be her year to live up to the family name, and her chances looked good. She had tried out for cheerleading and made the squad, and she had caught the eye of the handsomest boy on the football team.

Then there was the accident. The chance of cheerleading seemed lost to her forever. There could be no excitement, no popularity, now. Even swimming, once her favorite pastime, became a chore—a recommended exercise in the long recovery process.

Ryndy was convinced that it was fate, that her only chance was past. And all she wanted now was for everyone to leave her alone, to let her be the one girl in her family who never quite made it at anything. . . .

The Family Name

by JAN WASHBURN

cover by Lee Styles

 A WHITMAN BOOK
Western Publishing Company, Inc.
Racine, Wisconsin

Contents

1 · The Trouble With Sisters

Ryndy Drews stared miserably at the wall clock above the chalkboard. It was only two thirty. How could one class period last so long?

Cheerleader tryouts were at three o'clock, but she would never live through that next half hour. *If I don't have a nervous breakdown first, I'm going to get lead poisoning from chewing on this pencil,* Ryn decided. She laid the pencil firmly on her desk.

She shifted uncomfortably in her chair and tried to focus her attention on her teacher. Mrs.

Davis was droning on in a flat, monotonous voice—something about the Pilgrims and their struggles in coming to America. Eleventh-grade American history was not Ryn's favorite subject —especially a dull review of the year's work— and the Florida sun was hot this muggy May afternoon. She dropped her chin into her hand and closed her eyes.

She could picture herself now in the short, flared, orange and white skirt and a white cheer-leading sweater with a big orange *C* for Coral Cove High, leaping into the air in a soaring jump, while the crowd roared enthusiastically. Brad Hamilton would have to notice her then. He would come limping over at the end of the game, his orange football jersey torn and caked with mud. He'd pull off his helmet, and that lock of dark hair would fall over his forehead. He'd take her hand, and those deep brown eyes would look into hers. "You did it, Ryndy," he would say. "I don't think I could have intercepted that touchdown pass without your cheers."

"Kathryn Drews!"

Startled, Ryndy jerked her head up and sent her history book sailing into the aisle with a bump of her elbow.

"Yes, ma'am," she gulped anxiously.

"That question was directed at you," Mrs. Davis snapped.

Question, Ryndy agonized. *What question?* She didn't dare ask Mrs. Davis to repeat. With her luck she would get a detention for daydreaming in class. Today, of all days, she could not stay after school.

Stalling, Ryndy cleared her throat a few times, trying to think. What had Mrs. Davis been talking about? It must have been something about where the Pilgrims had taken refuge before they sailed to America.

"Holland," she offered hopefully.

There was a deadly silence, followed by gasps of muffled laughter. Her classmates were in quiet hysterics. Jody, the class clown, had to make a big deal of it by falling out of his chair and literally rolling in the aisle.

Mrs. Davis was furious. Her lips, purple with rage, trembled so that she could barely speak. "No, Kathryn," she hissed through clenched teeth, "Holland was not one of the thirteen original colonies."

Ryndy shriveled down into her chair, wondering if there were some way she could crawl unnoticed over to the window and quietly fall two floors to the patio.

She could see the derisive sneer on the face of Miss Smart Aleck, Allyson Bryant. Allyson was mouthing the word *dum-dum* for everyone to see.

But Mrs. Davis wasn't through. "Kathryn," she said grimly, "are you related to Virginia Drews?"

"Yes, ma'am," Ryndy mumbled. "She's my oldest sister."

Mrs. Davis shook her head in total disbelief and turned away. Ryndy stared numbly at her desk, sensing the ridicule in the thirty pairs of eyes that were fixed on her.

"Class, please start on tomorrow's reading assignment," Mrs. Davis announced weakly, as though she had despaired of any further attempts at oral recitation for the day.

Without lifting her head, Ryndy rescued her history book from the floor and opened it to the assigned chapter.

Why did Mrs. Davis have to drag Ginny's name into this? It was bad enough being a nothing, without teachers constantly reminding you of how great your sisters were.

Virginia was the brain of the Drews family. She was doing atomic research at the University of Rochester while working for her doctorate.

Ginny had never had anything but A's in any subject in her whole life. It had been eight long years since Ginny graduated from Coral Cove High, but the teachers were still talking about her genius.

After Virginia came Vicky, the family beauty. Vicky was an old married woman now, expecting her first child, but she was prettier than ever. Vicky had won every beauty contest at Coral Cove High and at the University of Florida— Homecoming Queen, Fraternity Sweetheart, Calendar Cover Girl. The high point of her career had been as queen of the Orange Bowl, enthroned on a gorgeous float, reigning over the big New Year's Eve parade on nationwide television. Boys that Vicky had never heard of called her at all hours of the night and wrote mushy letters to her. She could have been a model if she hadn't chosen to marry Russ instead.

Next in line was Val, the personality kid. Val was little and lively and talented. She had a sweet, husky singing voice and a light touch with a guitar. She had been captain of the cheerleaders and vice-president of her class, voted "Most Popular Girl" and "Best All-Around" at Coral Cove. Now she was repeating her triumphs at Florida State University.

Brains, beauty, personality, and talent. The Drews girls had them all. *And then I came along,* Ryndy groaned inwardly. When the family was already complete in every way, little Ryn had to arrive on the scene.

And there was nothing left for me, she thought gloomily. Of course, her older sisters adored her. They had fussed over her like three little mothers with a live baby doll, fighting for the privilege of dressing her, reading her stories, and spoon-feeding her. All she had to do was wave a baby hand, and three willing slaves rushed to her command. *It's a wonder I even learned to feed myself,* Ryndy sighed.

Her sisters didn't seem to notice the lack of talent in the baby of the family. They didn't really expect anything of her. She wasn't supposed to do anything. She was supposed to sit back and be the family's pampered pet.

But I'm real, Ryn thought grimly. *I'm not a toy. I want to be someone, too.*

Ryn began a dismal mental inventory. *I surely haven't got Vicky's looks.* Vicky's long hair was strawberry blond and her eyes a startling green. Ryndy's eyes couldn't decide whether to be amber or brown, and her hair was a sort of nondescript honey color, streaked by the sun. She wore it tied up in two ponytails to keep it out of the way. She knew it wasn't a very glamorous style, but no matter what she did with it, it never looked like Vicky's. Where Vicky had curves, Ryndy had straight lines. And her legs were too long. *Why couldn't I at least have been little and cute, like Val, or tall and regal, like Ginny?*

And I don't have Ginny's brains, she told herself. *That's for sure. I'll be lucky to get a high school diploma, let alone a doctorate.* Vicky and Val had been regulars on the honor roll, too, but Ryn's report card showed a monotonous row of C's, with an occasional B—perhaps even a D— thrown in for variety. In her freshman and sophomore years, her grades had been so miserable that she hadn't even been eligible to try out for cheerleading.

And personality like Val? Not a chance. Val could charm a smile out of a statue, but Ryn froze in the presence of a stranger, especially a good-looking boy. Her tongue stuck to the roof of her mouth and her vocal cords solidified at the very idea of speaking to an attractive male.

It's a wonder the family didn't just put me in a clothes basket and leave me on the doorstep at the orphanage, Ryn thought. *Or maybe that's where they found me in the first place. How else did I ever wind up in the Drews family?*

Here she was, at the end of her junior year, a total nothing. In September she would be a senior, and what did she have to show for it? Her presence at Coral Cove High had had all the impact of a falling marshmallow.

She *had* to make the cheerleading squad today. It was her last chance to be one of the Drews girls, not just a bumbling little stranger who happened to have the same last name.

She couldn't go on forever reading her sisters' newspaper clippings, dusting their trophies and their bulging scrapbooks, and applauding their successes, without adding something to the family laurels.

They're going to be proud of me, too, she vowed to herself. She sneaked another quick glance at the clock. Two fifty. Just ten more minutes.

She felt her heart beating faster and gripped her book tightly to steady her trembling hands. *It's now or never,* she thought grimly. *I've got to make the cheerleading squad.*

Uneasily, Ryndy fingered the big number twenty pinned to her gym suit. Wedged into the corner by her locker, she felt like a stowaway on the *Titanic*. The locker room was so crowded, she couldn't even bend over to tie her sneakers.

Someone wearing a number fifty stepped heavily on her toe. "Fifty!" Ryn gasped, forgetting the pain. Fifty girls trying out? But there were only eight openings on the squad.

Anxiously she searched the faces in the crowd. Where was GoGo? Her best friend was always her moral support in moments of crisis. She caught a glimpse of a dark head on the far side of the room. "Excuse me. . . . Pardon me." Ryn elbowed her way through the milling bodies.

GoGo was calmly pulling a comb through her hair in front of the long mirror. How could she be so nonchalant? Ryn tugged at her sleeve. "Aren't you nervous, Go?"

Go made a wry face in the mirror. "Of course not," she answered. "I just put my gym suit on backward for good luck."

Ryn tried to smile, but a sharp elbow was drilling into her ribs. "Look at this mob, Go. Do you think we've got any chance at all?"

Glumly GoGo surveyed the chattering crowd. "If they put fifty on the squad, we're in."

The cheerleader captain, Shannon O'Neill, appeared in the doorway, megaphone in hand. Shannon was a dark-haired pixie with Irish blue eyes and a voice like a tugboat captain's. "Okay, girls," she roared. "Report to the patio."

GoGo joined the stampede toward the door, but Ryn stood staring vacantly at the spot where Shannon had been. "GoGo," she choked. "I can't go through with it. I absolutely cannot do it."

Go stopped in flight and looked back over her shoulder. "What are you talking about, Ryn? Come on."

"Go, my sister Val was cheerleading captain when Shannon was a ninth grader. Val picked Shannon for the team."

"Well, that's good, isn't it?"

"No, it isn't!" Ryn protested. "Shannon knows I'm Val's sister. She'll expect me to be so great and—"

GoGo seized Ryndy's arm and dragged her through the door.

Outside, Shannon was waving her arms like a symphony conductor. "Line up along the walk by number," she shouted. "Start with Number One over here. Please remain in place until your number is called."

Go was wearing the number twenty-one. She seemed to know where she was going, so Ryn stumbled blindly along in her wake.

Suddenly, though, Go stopped in her tracks,

and Ryndy plowed into her back.

"What's the matter?" Ryn gasped.

"Get a load of Number Nineteen!" Go pointed.

Above the number nineteen was the smirking face of Allyson Bryant. "Oh, no," Ryn groaned. "If she makes the squad, I'll burn my student ID card."

But Allyson was waiting to greet them with a malicious smile. "Well, Ryndy," she inquired saccharinely, "when are you moving to Holland, our fifty-first state?"

Ryndy felt the color rushing to her face, but she managed a sweet smile. "On the day you say something pleasant to somebody, Allyson."

Allyson snorted and turned away, flipping her long blond hair in disdain. Go gave Ryndy a huge wink.

But Ryndy had more important things to worry about than Allyson's sharp tongue. Uneasily she studied the faces of the judges. They were seated in a semicircle on the patio, facing the long line of contestants. They looked as solemn as a row of Supreme Court justices. There were the eight seniors, including Shannon, who had been members of the squad the past year, and eight faculty members. Ryn was relieved to see that her history teacher was not among them. *Mrs. Davis wouldn't pick me to empty the pencil sharpener today,* Ryn thought.

"All ready, Number One," Shannon announced. A little redhead moved up in front of the judges, and the trials were under way.

"Give us a 'Fight, Team, Fight,'" Shannon called.

Ryndy grasped one of her ponytails and twisted it nervously as the redhead began her routine. This was going to be a rough afternoon. Maybe it had been a mistake to even try out. She knew her parents hoped that she would give up the whole idea. Her sisters were blind to her faults, but her parents were well aware of her shortcomings. They had smiled sympathetically when she first mentioned trying out, but she had caught the glances they exchanged. She knew that look and had learned to interpret it: *Poor little Ryn, the runt of the litter. She'll only get her heart broken, but there's no way to stop her from trying.*

Ryn realized she had tied her ponytail in a complete knot. She forced her hands down to her sides. Just because she was dying of fright, she wasn't going to let everyone here know about it. She tugged absently at her fingers. The line was moving so slowly. It would take forever to judge fifty girls.

She watched Number Twelve execute a perfect cartwheel and felt her heart parachuting down toward her knees. *They're all so good,* she thought.

If the judges only knew how much it meant to her to make the squad. If wanting something badly enough was the secret, she should be their choice for all eight places. But the faces of the judges revealed nothing. They watched each girl intently, scribbling hasty notes on pads of paper, but their expressions never changed. Their faces might as well have been painted on the wall.

"Number Nineteen."

Ryndy jumped, startled back to the moment. Nineteen was Allyson. As Allyson moved to the front, Ryndy could feel her own breathing completely stop.

"Give us a 'T-E-A-M,' " Shannon ordered.

Allyson looked perfectly at ease. She dropped confidently to one knee and began the familiar chant in a throaty voice. Her arms were swinging with perfect snap and precision. *I wonder if Allyson has any older sisters,* Ryn thought.

"Do 'Go, Coral Cove,' " Shannon called to Allyson.

Ryndy took a firm hold on her ponytail. "Go, Coral Cove" was the most difficult of the required cheers. It demanded perfect timing, with high, straight-legged kicks, and it ended with a full split.

But Allyson, her long blond hair swinging behind her, was kicking as easily as a Radio City Rockette. Ryndy turned around to Go and rolled her eyes in anguish. "She's terrific, Go," she whispered.

GoGo drew her brows together in a frown. "Have you ever thought about running away from home?" she suggested.

Allyson attempted to finish the cheer with a deep split. For a moment she seemed to lose her balance. Ryndy felt GoGo's excited punch. "That split wasn't so great," Go whispered eagerly, her voice rising on a note of hope.

"No," Ryndy agreed, "but no one else has done a really great split, either."

"Yeah." GoGo subsided in despair.

Well, at least we tried, Ryn consoled herself. She had never worked so hard for anything in all the seventeen years of her life—memorizing cheers when she should have been memorizing Latin conjugations, practicing cartwheels and splits with Go till they both ached in muscles they didn't know they had.

But the judges didn't care if you had been practicing for forty years and your ancestors on both sides had been cheerleaders at Washington's inauguration. You kicked and you jumped and you cheered well—or thumbs down.

Allyson was completing her trial with a cartwheel. Her legs just missed forming a perfect arc. One leg drooped ever so slightly. Ryn tried to smother an unsportsmanlike squeal of joy.

Head held high, Allyson was smiling as she walked back to her place in line, but Ryndy knew she wasn't satisfied with her showing. Did the judges expect absolute perfection?

"Number Twenty," came the call.

Ryndy's muscles turned to stone. She was Number Twenty, but no one could expect her to perform when rigor mortis was setting in.

"Move," Go whispered urgently, pushing her forward. "And smile."

Ryndy walked stiffly to the center of the circle. She had no idea whether or not she was smiling. There was no feeling in the muscles of her face, and her feet seemed to be clumping along about two or three inches above the ground.

"Give us 'What D'ya Wanna Bet,'" Shannon called out.

Ryndy stared blankly at the blur of faces. Somewhere in the back of her head the small faint voice of reason was trying to make itself heard. *What's the matter with you?* the voice demanded. *Val wouldn't let this shake her up. She would put up her chin, flash a big smile, and go.*

But I'm not Val, she protested. *I'm her clumsy kid sister, and I've got too many left feet.*

So what are you going to do? the voice argued. *Go through with this, or tell Shannon that Val Drews's sister is so petrified she can't even move?*

Ryn straightened her back, wrenched her mouth into a smile, and began. At first her motions felt wooden and artificial, and then gradually she began to feel the rhythm of the cheer. Somehow the right motions began to come. Even the drum major's strut did not present its usual challenge.

The cheer ended with a soaring jump and a forward lunge. She flung herself through the air and then waited, tense with expectation, for the judges to mark their scorecards.

Keep smiling, she told herself, clenching her teeth.

" 'Go, Coral Cove,' " called Shannon.

This is the tough one, Ryn thought. *But*

Shannon knows you're Val's sister. You've got to try. Determined, she swung her legs up in the high kicks. Somehow they felt right, her back arched, her toes pointed. And then the split. Ryndy leaped forward, stretching her legs to the fullest, extending her arms for balance.

I think it was okay, she thought, almost daring to hope. She got to her feet, watching the tops of the judges' heads as they scribbled their notes. She would have given two weeks' allowance to see those pages.

"Now do your cartwheel, Number Twenty," called Shannon.

Just one more stunt. Ryndy drew a deep breath, pulled back her shoulders, and swung herself into an arc.

Had her legs drooped? She wasn't sure. She waited for the word of dismissal with her fists clenched at her sides.

"Thank you, Number Twenty. That's all," Shannon said.

Ryndy let out her breath in a long sigh. *How was it?* She glanced anxiously back at Go.

Go formed a big O with thumb and forefinger.

Go's satisfied, Ryn thought in relief. *I guess it wasn't too bad.* She stumbled wearily to her place in line again behind Allyson.

"Number Twenty-One," Shannon was calling. It was GoGo's turn.

Ryndy forgot her weariness and watched expectantly as GoGo stepped forward.

"Try 'Two Bits,' Number Twenty-One."

Ryndy crossed her fingers as GoGo began her cheer. But something was wrong. Go was forgetting to smile. She looked as grim and serious as the dean of girls. She wasn't showing any of the snap she had in Ryndy's backyard.

"Come on, Go," Ryn whispered earnestly. "Do it like you did at home."

"That moose doesn't really expect to make the team, does she?" Allyson was saying sarcastically. "She's about as graceful as a bull alligator."

"GoGo's all right," Ryndy snapped angrily. "She's just nervous. She's as good as anyone here."

"Well, she'll never make it on her beauty, so she better start showing some style," Allyson sneered.

Ryndy clamped her jaws over the words she wanted to say. *If Allyson's face were as ugly as her disposition, she would have to wear a paper bag over her head.*

GoGo was doing the "Coral Cove Strut" now, but she just didn't have it. Ryndy felt tears welling up. Go was her best friend, but she would never make the squad with this performance.

GoGo drooped through a halfhearted effort at a cartwheel and trudged back to her place behind Ryndy. "Boy, I really goofed it," she mumbled.

"What happened, Go?" Ryndy groaned. "You know you can do much better than that."

"Oh, I don't know." Go's face was flushed with embarrassment. "I just disintegrate with all those judges staring at me."

"Why don't you try out for the football team?" Allyson Bryant put in sweetly. "You've got the build for it."

"Why don't you get off your broomstick?" Ryndy retorted. But Allyson was already turning away to watch the next contestant.

GoGo stared silently at her feet. Her broad-shouldered, athletic figure was a touchy subject.

The sun seemed to grow hotter as the judges worked their way down the line. The humidity pushed down on the school buildings and the athletic field like the cover on a gigantic pressure cooker.

Ryn was sure that they would never complete the first round of trials, but at last the judges began to call some of the girls back in groups of two or three for a review. Ryndy was called a second time and then a third. She had to strut

again, jump again, do her cartwheel and her split.
She was unaware of everyone and everything
now, except GoGo's voice whispering intently,
"Smile, Ryn. Smile. You're doing great."

Allyson, too, was called back several times, but
GoGo's number was not requested again. Ryn
felt as though she ought to offer some words of
consolation, but GoGo was smiling cheerfully, as
though she had already accepted her fate.

"That's it, girls," Shannon announced.
"Thanks, everybody, for coming out today and
being so patient. The names of those who made
the squad will be posted on the sports bulletin
board tomorrow morning."

Ryndy felt her knees starting to sag. "Tomorrow morning! Oh, Go, it might as well be next
year."

Go laughed. "You'll live. Maybe I'm preju-
diced, but you were the best one out there."

"I wish you had been one of the judges."

The girls trudged back to the locker room to
change. The bubbling chatter had diminished to
weary whispers now. Ryn and Go moved slowly
as they started toward home, seeking the shade
of the palms along the sidewalk.

"You know, I really don't care that I'm not
going to make it," Go confided, "but I sure hope

old Fork-Tongue Bryant doesn't. She's so hopelessly conceited already."

"But she was good, Go. You have to admit
it. And she's pretty, too."

"So's a saber-toothed tiger."

Ryn nodded sadly. "Well, tomorrow will get
here eventually, I suppose."

"Yeah, that's what the calendar says. Hey, by
the way, are you going to the hospital with us
Saturday?"

"Saturday?" Ryn gasped. "Oh, the Coralteens."
Their youth fellowship from church had voted to
begin visiting the children in the pediatrics ward
at least once a month. "I had forgotten all about
it," she admitted. She didn't need to tell Go that
she had forgotten everything else for the past two
weeks except the date and time of cheerleader
tryouts.

"Reverend Carter asked us to meet in the
lobby at two thirty. Tom's going to bring all
the stuff we collected in Sunday school."

Ryn tried to put Allyson and Shannon and the
judges out of her mind and think about what
Go was saying. "Do you think those kids really
like having a bunch of people come in and make
a fuss over them?"

"I guess so," Go reflected. "I mean, if *you* had

been lying around in a hospital for a couple of weeks or maybe even months, you'd be glad to see *Frankenstein* if he was all loaded down with books and games and stuff."

Ryn smiled. "Are you comparing Tom Cantrell to Frankenstein?"

Go laughed. "Well, Tom makes a good president, but he'll never win any beauty prizes."

They had reached Ryn's driveway, and she realized for the first time that she was about to collapse from starvation. "I'll be there Saturday," she promised. "But keep your fingers crossed tonight, Go."

As Go vanished behind the hedge, Ryn waved a good-bye and trudged wearily up the front walk. The mail was lying on the table in the front hall, and Ryn glanced at it disinterestedly. Her spirits lifted as she noticed a little package with her name on it.

The package was tiny—there was hardly room for the address. Ryn broke the string and tore eagerly at the wrappings. Inside was a small white box.

"What on earth?" she murmured, tugging at the lid. There, enthroned in satin, like a precious gem, was a tiny gold megaphone—a trinket for a cheerleader's charm bracelet. The little note inside was in Vicky's handwriting. "To the new sweetheart of Coral Cove High."

Quick tears sprang to Ryn's eyes. *Oh, Vicky,* she thought miserably, *I'm not the school sweetheart type. What if I don't even make the squad?*

2 · Suddenly You're Popular!

"Ryndy, don't gobble your food that way. We'll have to have your stomach relined." Ryndy stopped in the middle of a mouthful as her mother rescued the milk bottle from the danger zone by her elbow. Ryn thought she had been concealing the anxiety she felt, but her mother could always read the signs.

"I've got to hurry, Mom," she argued through her toast. "The list of names will be posted this morning."

"Well, you won't be leading any cheers with

an overworked gullet," her mother announced
firmly.

Ryn made herself slow down, chewing thoughtfully as she watched her mother squeezing oranges. Mom didn't look old enough to have a
daughter as old as Ginny, but she seemed to have
completely forgotten what it was like to be seventeen. They shared the same name—Kathryn.
Mom was Kathy, so she was Ryn, but all resem-
blance ended with the name. Mom must have
been one of the "in" crowd, like Vicky or Val or
Ginny, always on top, always a winner. None of
them would ever understand what it was like
being the oddball, wondering if you were going
to be the only Drews in the history of Coral Cove
High to be a total disaster.

Had Ginny ever been scared to death of a
test—so petrified by the questions that the facts
just congealed in her brain? Had Vicky ever
yearned in vain to have a boy notice her—a very
special boy like Brad Hamilton, who didn't know
she was alive? Had Val lain awake all night after
the cheerleading trials, afraid even to look at the
list of names posted the next day? Did any of
them have any idea what it was like to hope and
try and never make it to the top?

A piercing whistle penetrated her thoughts.

"That's GoGo. I've got to run." Ryn leaped to her feet, sending her chair back with a clatter.

"Ryndy," her mother called.

Ryn stopped in flight. Her mother was looking at her wistfully, as though there was something she wanted to say. Ryn waited expectantly.

"Ryn, try not to be too disappointed if you don't make it," her mother said.

"I won't," Ryn insisted with a reassuring smile. *I'll just crawl into the nearest land-crab hole and stay there for the rest of my life,* she told herself.

She burst into the front hall, colliding with her father in the doorway. "Oh, Dad," she gasped. "Sorry, I've got to fly."

"Good heavens! What's the commotion? Are they burning all the textbooks this morning?"

"Got to see if I made the squad, Dad." Ryn snatched up her books, waved a good-bye, and pushed open the front door, all in one motion.

As she hurried down the walk to meet Go, she could still hear her father's voice behind her. "What on earth is Ryndy so excited about? She doesn't really expect to make the squad, does she?"

"My family!" Ryndy groaned.

Go was waiting for her at the end of the walk. "Hi, Ryn. Got all your nails chewed off?"

Good old GoGo. She thinks I have a chance, anyway. "I'm a wreck," Ryn confided.

"Honestly, Ryn, I told you, you can't miss."

"Just keep saying that over and over, and I'll believe it when I read it on the bulletin board. Let's move."

Their usual gait was a casual stroll, but this morning Ryn made GoGo march double time. "Come on, Go," she urged. "We'll be the last ones in the whole school to know. Hurry up. You're not even trying to walk fast."

"Have mercy, Ryn," Go pleaded. "This chemistry book weighs forty-eight pounds."

It was not quite a mile to the high school, and Ryn felt herself aging ten years with every step.

The sports bulletin board was at the end of a long walkway near the gym. Ryn could see the crowd of girls craning their necks to get a look at the list. She tugged anxiously at Go's arm.

"Kathryn. Kathryn Drews."

Ryndy stopped, startled, and spun around. No one ever called her by her full name.

"It's the principal," Go gasped. "Mr. Martin."

In her three years at Coral Cove High, Ryndy had seen the principal in the corridors and at all the school assemblies, but she had never talked to him face-to-face. She didn't realize he even knew her by name. What on earth had she done to make him suddenly pick her out of the crowd? She tried to read some clue in his lined forehead and bushy eyebrows.

"You're Virginia's sister, aren't you?" Mr. Martin asked.

"Yes, sir," she admitted hesitantly.

"You know, I had Virginia as a student in my physics class before I became principal."

"Yes, sir." Ryn struggled to keep her attention on Mr. Martin while the bulletin board beckoned at the fringes of her vision. She couldn't just turn around and run when the principal was trying to talk to her.

"Wonderful girl," Mr. Martin was saying reminiscently. "The finest student I've ever had. Of course, I never had the opportunity to have Victoria or Valerie as students, but I've heard wonderful things about both of them."

"Yes, sir," Ryn mumbled.

"I wanted to tell you that the YWCA has asked me to recommend several college girls for their summer camp staff. Of course, Drews was the first name that came into my head. Do you think Valerie would be interested? I'm sure she'd enjoy it. Pass the word along to her, and tell her to drop them a line."

"Yes, Mr. Martin. Thank you. I'll tell her." Ryn shifted her weight uneasily from one foot to the other.

"How is Val doing at the University?" Apparently Mr. Martin was in no hurry to end the conversation.

"Oh, fine. She loves it. She's very happy there." Ryn began edging backward along the walk.

"And Virginia's doing atomic research, as I understand."

"Yes, sir, in Rochester, New York."

"Well, I was very pleased to find that we have another Drews girl here to carry on the family tradition."

Ryn could feel her face turning scarlet. "I . . . I hope . . . I can," she stammered. "I was just going down to see if I made the cheerleading squad."

"Oh, I mustn't detain you, then. Good luck, young lady." Mr. Martin turned away, beaming, obviously convinced that the halls of Coral Cove High were brightened by the presence of another Ginny. Apparently he hadn't checked Ryn's academic record. She hoped it wouldn't be too much of a shock to his system when he learned the horrible truth.

She turned and sprinted down the walk. *I'm*

going to change my name, she thought desperately, *to Mary Smith.* Surely no one would expect a Mary Smith to be anything special. Ryn was out of breath as she skidded to a halt at the end of the walk.

The jostling bodies formed an impenetrable barrier around the bulletin board, but Ryn could see that GoGo had maneuvered her way to the front of the mob. There were times when a sturdy build was a definite advantage.

"Go!" she shouted. "What does it say?"

Go's head appeared above the throng. She was grinning broadly. "I told you you made it," she shouted. "Right at the head of the list."

Ryn felt her knees grow limp. *I made it,* she thought weakly. She stood grinning vacantly at nothing. She had actually made the squad. But it didn't seem possible. She felt a nudge of worry. *I want to see it for myself.*

The crowd shifted slightly, and Ryn felt GoGo's hand pulling her through an opening. "There!" Go pronounced triumphantly.

It was there, all right, in black and white. Ryn stared, fascinated, at the printed words. Kathryn Drews. She tried to picture her mother and father hearing the news. "Ryndy made it? Our little Ryndy made the cheerleading squad?"

Her sisters would accept the news matter-of-factly. Of course she made it. Their precious baby sister should have nothing but the best, whether she deserved it or not.

But I must have earned it, Ryn told herself. *I must have been one of the best ones.* But who else had made the squad? She had been so wrapped up in her own success that she hadn't even thought about Go. Quickly she ran her eye down the list, seeking the name Gloria Olivera. She felt some of the joy slipping away. Go hadn't made it.

Another list, the names of the alternates, caught her eye. These were the girls who would take over when a regular cheerleader moved away or was dropped because of grades or something. Go's name wasn't there, either; but Allyson Bryant was listed as first alternate.

Ryn pointed to the name and raised her eyebrows at Go.

Go nodded grimly. They needed no words to express their opinion.

The girls behind them were trying to push to the front, and reluctantly Go and Ryndy squeezed out into the fresh air again.

"Gee, Go, I'm so sorry you didn't make it, too. It would be lots more fun."

Go laughed easily. "Well, you can bet Coach Helgesen won't be sorry. He hates to have his swimmers go out for any other activity. If he had his way, we'd all be padlocked to the pool deck between workouts."

"So this is Ryndy Drews," a deep voice interrupted. "This is the girl I want to meet."

Without turning around, without seeing his face, Ryn knew by the voice who it was. She felt as though the whole world had screeched to a stop and started whirling in the other direction. She thought the day had reached its climax when she read her name on that bulletin board, but now— Breathless, she turned around.

He was smiling, extending his hand. "I'm Brad Hamilton. Hello, Ryndy."

Ryn put out her hand like a mechanical doll, unable to utter a sound. Brad's crinkly black hair and laughing brown eyes had been floating in her head since the day she had first seen him on the rostrum as president of the junior class. An impartial survey would probably have shown that nine out of ten girls at Coral Cove were crazy about Brad Hamilton—and Ryn couldn't think of a single word to say to him.

"Congratulations," he said with a smile.

"Thanks," she croaked weakly.

"Now I've got to sweat out some trials, too. I'm running for student council president, you know."

Ryndy nodded, hypnotized.

"I'm hoping to get the cheerleaders and some of the other popular girls on my side for the campaign."

Ryndy continued to stare at him. Other popular girls? Was he classifying her with the popular girls? No more than a hundred students at Coral Cove even knew Ryndy Drews existed. In a school of twenty-five hundred students, she just blended into the chalkboards.

"Can I count on your support, Ryndy? It would be a big help to me."

"Well . . . I . . . yes . . . I mean . . . sure." Ryndy stumbled helplessly over her own tongue.

"That's great." Brad grinned. "What I have in mind is—"

"Oh, Brad Hamilton, there you are." Allyson Bryant hurried up to them, her blond hair twitching with impatience. She seized Brad's arm possessively. "I've been hunting all over school for you."

Brad didn't seem to mind the interruption. "Nice going, Al. I see you made alternate."

"Thanks," Allyson retorted sharply. "I would

have done better if I had a little pull with Shannon, like some of the others." She flashed a syrupy smile at Ryndy.

Ryn tried to open her mouth to counter the insinuation, but Allyson was going on. "Listen, I've got a terrific idea for your campaign." Slyly, but firmly, Allyson was turning Brad around, leading him away from the others. "Now, tell me what you think of this."

Ryndy stood there, helpless, watching them in astonishment.

"I'll talk to you later, Ryndy," Brad called over his shoulder. "Nice to meet you."

"Well, now how do you like that?" GoGo exclaimed.

Ryndy continued to stare.

"Ryn, close your mouth and put your eyes back in your head. You look as though you've been struck by lightning."

Go's words brought Ryndy out of her trance. She realized she had let Brad disappear without uttering a single coherent sentence. "Oh, Go," she sighed, "I'm hopeless. All year I've waited for a chance to meet Brad Hamilton. So what happens? He says hello, and I go into cardiac arrest. Why didn't you poke me or something?"

"Allyson was saying enough for both of you,"

Go snapped. "I thought she was going to put a hammerlock on him."

"She's not very subtle," Ryndy agreed. "But do you think it's true, what she said about having pull with Shannon? Do you think that's why I was chosen?"

"Oh, baloney," Go retorted. "She just can't admit that you're better than she is."

Ryndy mulled that over. "Well, she seems to be a lot better at talking to boys than I am. I come all unglued when a guy says hello. I can't even come up with a brilliant reply like 'How are you?' "

"I know," Go sympathized. "Hey, it's almost time for the bell. We better get moving."

"Mmmm," Ryn agreed dreamily. "What do you suppose Brad wants me to do for him in his campaign?"

"I don't imagine he'll ask you to make any speeches," GoGo assured her.

Ryn moved aimlessly in the direction of her locker. It seemed as though the rest of the day should be declared a school holiday. How could anyone expect her to learn anything today?

Shannon O'Neill caught her arm as she wandered dreamily toward her homeroom. "Hey, Ryndy, congratulations! I'm so glad you made it." She thrust a note into Ryndy's hand. "This is an invitation to a little party at my house Saturday night," Shannon explained. "I'm inviting all the cheerleaders, old and new, and some of the boys from the football team, like Brad. It's just informal—cookout and records and stuff. Can you make it?"

"I wouldn't miss it for the world!" Ryndy was ecstatic. "Thanks so much, Shannon." The bell for the first class was ringing impatiently, but Ryndy stood lost in the middle of the loggia, oblivious to the world. It was finally happening, the way she had always dreamed. The clumsy old caterpillar was turning into a social butterfly. Maybe there would be another glamorous Drews girl at Coral Cove, after all.

3 · Last Cookie on the Plate

Ryndy stood breathless at the edge of the patio, surveying the gay scene before her. Shannon's home was beautiful. Like many homes in Coral Cove, it was on a waterway, and the colored lights strung through the trees and along the dock were reflected in the water.

The patio was jammed with young people crowding around the grill or trying to dance while juggling cold drinks and hamburgers.

Apparently dear Allyson had arrived early and appointed herself Shannon's assistant hostess. She was serving the hamburgers, treating every boy to a flirtatious fluttering of her eyelashes along with his mustard and ketchup.

But Ryndy wasn't interested in Allyson. Her eyes searched through the laughing faces. All the girls seemed to be here—the twelve old cheerleaders, the eight new members, and the four alternates. And she recognized most of the boys —the football players, the senior class president, the student council officers, all of the "inner circle." But where was Brad?

Ryn was determined that she wasn't going to make a fool of herself tonight. She had spent the afternoon selecting just the right outfit to wear. She had found a white sundress that really set off her dark tan.

And she wasn't going to be tongue-tied, either. She had a whole list of sparkling remarks and questions, guaranteed to flatter a boy and give him a chance to brag about himself.

"Look out, you peasants. Cold stuff coming through."

Ryndy stiffened at the sound of Brad's voice. He was prancing across the patio with a case of soft drinks balanced on his shoulder. He executed a few fancy steps while the bottles swayed perilously, then swung the case safely down to the picnic table beside the grill.

"Don't ask me to recommend you for a job in a china shop, Brad," Shannon groaned. She turned back to the grill and then noticed Ryndy, standing in the shadows. "Hey, Ryn, come get something to eat before these vultures devour everything, including the charcoal."

Brad turned around, his face alight with interest. "Why, Miss Ryndy," he drawled, sweeping his arm in a low bow, like a courtly Southern gentleman, "don't you look purty tonight."

Ryn felt her prepared speeches flutter away like uncaged birds. "Thank you," she mumbled incoherently. There should be some cute remark she could make now, but her tongue felt as though it had just doubled in size.

"Take a hamburger, Ryn." Shannon waved a hand toward the laden table. "And pay no attention to Gentleman Jim. He's already playing the politician."

"Politicians kiss babies," Brad observed, rolling his eyes expressively at Ryndy.

Ryndy could feel a blush starting at her toes and creeping right up over her face. *Say something,* she told herself desperately.

"You must have a Coke opened by my own loving hands," Brad announced. "Now, you just sit right down here and let me take care of you."

Ryn dropped helplessly into a lounge chair as Brad insisted on waiting on her. He heaped her plate with potato salad, baked beans, hamburger, and pickles and presented it as though he were offering the crown jewels.

Ryndy forced her face into a gay smile, still racking her brain to recall just one of the amusing remarks she had stored up.

Brad heaped another plate for himself and plopped down on the foot of her chair. "Your servant awaits Your Majesty's bidding." He bowed his head humbly.

"Her Majesty bids you to quit yakking and eat," Shannon put in.

Now, why didn't I say something like that? Ryndy thought helplessly. She could toss wisecracks at Go or her other girl friends without a moment's thought, but the sight of Brad rendered her totally speechless.

But Brad seemed unaware of her mute state. He was following Shannon's advice and devouring his food enthusiastically, snapping his fingers to the beat of the music.

Ryndy took a dainty bite of her hamburger. She loved to eat, and hamburger was near the top of her list of favorites, but she didn't want Brad to think she was a complete glutton. She always worried that people would think a girl who was almost five feet eight had to have the appetite of a starving elephant.

The food temporarily eliminated the problem of conversation, and Ryn realized that her brain was finally sending out a few feeble signals. *Val would get things started by asking Brad about his campaign,* she thought hopefully. She tried to imitate her sister's light, teasing voice. "How are the politics going?" she choked.

"Oh, great!" Brad turned to her eagerly. "We can start campaigning officially on Monday—you know, putting up posters and stuff. Then Tuesday there's an assembly, so we can all make speeches and tell everyone what really great leaders we'd make."

"What can I do to help?" Ryn was surprised at the tone of her own voice. It really sounded like Val's.

"Anything you do would be a help." Brad moved closer to her on the lounge chair.

"I'm not the least bit artistic." Ryn was groping for words, but Brad looked interested. "I could make some campaign buttons."

"Hey, that would be great!"

"Let's see. You need a slogan." Ryn began to

get excited about the prospects. "How about 'Brad's our lad!'"

"Good, good," he laughed. "Or, 'Don't be mad—vote for Brad!'"

"'It's the fad—you're "in" with Brad.'"

"'Get off your pad and go with Brad.'"

It turned into a contest. For each slogan Brad proposed, Ryn came back with a topper. Why had she been so nervous? This was easy.

"I've got it," she shouted triumphantly. "'Hey, Daddy-o, vote for Braddy-o.'"

Brad whooped with delight.

Suddenly Ryn caught sight of Allyson looming up behind him. She looked as though she were ready for battle, but as Brad turned around, her lips suddenly curved into a beguiling smile.

"Brad Hamilton, you've got to come dance with me. Honestly, there's not another boy here that knows his right foot from his left."

Brad seemed flattered by her attention. "Why, Miss Bryant," he drawled, falling back into his Southern-gentleman routine. "I declare, I thought you'd never ask me."

Ryn felt her confidence vanishing as Brad stood up. She thought she had completely captivated him, yet here he was, ready to dance away as though she didn't exist.

Suddenly he seemed to remember her and hesitated. He glanced back apologetically.

"Oh, Ryndy doesn't mind—do you, Ryn?" Allyson's voice was stickily sweet, but her eyes flashed a threat.

There was nothing for Ryn to do but smile and nod agreement, as though she hadn't the slightest interest in Brad's company. He saluted her as they turned toward the dance floor. " 'Don't be sad—stay glad with Brad.' "

Ryn gritted her teeth in a brilliant smile. *It's just too bad that Brad's been had,* she thought bitterly.

She felt her old inferiority complex rising to the surface as she gathered up their dishes and carried them back to the serving table. She hoped that no one else was aware of what had happened, but Shannon was eyeing her sympathetically. "Cheer up, Ryn. If Allyson had any more brass, they'd have to use her for a plumbing fixture."

"Oh, she doesn't bother me." Ryn wished she meant what she was saying. "But why does Brad let her lead him around like her pet poodle?"

"Sometimes it's questionable who's leading whom," Shannon suggested.

"Need a hand with anything?" Ryn needed to be doing something, anything.

Shannon looked grateful. "How about watching the grill a minute? The kids have been bugging me to get out the badminton net. Just put the burgers on the platter when they're done."

As Shannon rushed away, Ryn took the spatula and gently prodded the meat. She didn't want to watch the dancers on the patio, but her eyes kept finding their way back to them, no matter where else she tried to look.

There were six or eight couples going through all the gyrations of the latest dance, but Brad and Allyson were far and away the best. They looked like professionals in a crowd of rank amateurs. *They must have danced together a lot,* she mused.

She forced her attention back to the grill. The burgers were ready, and she tried to concentrate on removing them from the fire, but it wasn't much of a task. Too soon the meat was carefully arranged on the dish. Ryn refilled the bowl of potato chips and rearranged the napkins, but there was really nothing else to do. Uneasily she looked around at the others. One group of boys was huddled in the corner, arguing the merits of the I formation. Others were helping Shannon set up the badminton set. Several of the girls were shuffling through the stack of records like enthusiastic disc jockeys, selecting the evening's program. Everyone seemed so relaxed and at ease.

There must be something she could do that would look casual and unplanned. Standing alone by the grill, she felt like the last cookie on the plate—the old maid.

In the distance she could make out a dim figure on the dock. One of the boys seemed to be sitting there alone, staring out across the canal. Maybe he felt as awkward as she did. If only she had the nerve to go out on the dock and strike up a conversation!

Val would, she thought. Val had a knack for picking out the strays in a crowd. She always seemed to find the lost souls floating on the fringes of a party and draw them in. Mimicking Val had helped her start her conversation with Brad. Maybe it could work again.

She straightened her shoulders and crossed the patio. She managed to brush past Allyson and Brad without giving them the satisfaction of a glance.

The boy on the dock didn't look up at the sound of her footsteps. She could feel her courage starting to dissolve. Maybe he didn't want company. But she couldn't turn around and go back to the dance floor now. Everyone had seen her walk out here.

She was just an arm's length from him now. She recognized the broad shoulders and the crop of white-blond hair. She had never met Dirk Hudson, but she knew the other football players called him "The Dutchman."

She had to say something now. She couldn't just stand there. Val would begin with something casual. "Oh, excuse me." Ryn tried to sound surprised. "I didn't realize there was anyone here."

Dirk turned and looked up at her. His face was dark with anger, but he didn't answer.

Ryn felt her knees starting to wobble. Why didn't he say something? Her voice was unsteady as she tried again. "I love to watch the water at night."

He continued to stare out into the darkness. She wanted to turn around and run, but there was no place to go. She was trapped. She had to give Val's method one more chance. Her voice was trembling. "You're Dirk Hudson, aren't you?"

He turned to look up at her again. His eyes were still hard with anger, but this time he spoke. "And you're Ryndy Drews."

Ryn nodded wordlessly. *I wish I were Val Drews,* she thought desperately, *because then I'd know what to say next.*

Dirk turned back to the water again, and Ryn clung shakily to the piling. What was the matter with him? She was just trying to be polite. He didn't have to act as though she were insulting him by saying hello.

Now she wasn't sure whether she was more frightened or angry. "You're quiet," she said, trying to keep the sharpness out of her voice.

But Dirk was getting to his feet. "Why don't you sit down and enjoy the dock?" he snapped. "I've had my turn." He turned abruptly and strode back toward the patio.

Ryn felt a sudden rush of tears. His rudeness was like a slap across the face. Still trembling, she sat down weakly on the edge of the dock and wondered if anyone would even miss her if she just slid into the water and swam quietly home.

You're a fool, she told herself. *You're not Vicky or Val, so why do you try to pretend that you are?*

The beat of the music washed over her and echoed back from the other side of the canal. She would make herself sit here for at least fifteen minutes. She liked to look at the water. She would show Brad Hamilton and Dirk Hudson that she didn't need either one of them.

"Hey, Ryn," Shannon's voice was calling from behind her. "We need another girl here for a game of doubles."

Ryn felt like a convict who had just been handed a reprieve from the governor. "Coming," she called back.

She ignored the crowd as she hurried to the badminton court. Shannon and her boyfriend, Glen, were ready on one side of the net while shy, lanky Tom Cantrell was waiting for a partner on the other. Ryn snatched up a racket and joined him.

They fought a blistering battle, and Ryn tried to concentrate all her attention on the game. In spite of herself, however, she found her glance slipping back to the dancers on the patio. Several times she noticed that Brad was looking in their direction, and she put on her best act, turning to smile up at Tom as though playing badminton with him were the most amusing and exciting thing she had done in ages.

Tom seemed confused by her unexpected attentions. Ryn had known Tom for years. He was president of their church group, the Coralteens, but Tom was puzzling. He could get up in front of a crowd and make a speech or conduct a meeting, but he was painfully shy with girls. Ryn suspected that he had a desperate crush on GoGo. Although they were on the swim team together, Tom seemed more tongue-tied than ever when Go was around.

Ryn realized what Shannon had done. Instead of playing a singles game with Glen, as she probably wanted to do, Shannon had arranged this doubles match to rescue the two misfits. Ryn was determined now to make the best of it. If Tom was her fate for the evening, that was fine with her.

As they battled for the winning point, Ryn realized that Brad was coming across the patio toward them. She threw herself more fiercely into the fray.

"Hey, Ryn," Brad called finally. "Are you going to play badminton all night? Aren't you ever going to come dance with me?"

Ryn made a diving swoop for a brilliant retrieve of the plummeting bird. "Can't stop now," she gasped. Seeing Brad waiting patiently for the end of the contest was the perfect prescription for her wounded pride. She fought determinedly to keep the duel going as long as possible, but at last Glen wiped them out with a jumping smash. "That's it!" she whooped.

"Come on now, Ryn. Let's dance," Brad urged.

Ryndy took her time putting away her racket. Just half an hour before, Brad had danced off with Allyson without a qualm. He could wait for her now.

"Thanks so much for the game, Tom." She really poured it on. "That was fun."

Tom glowed under her flattery. "Thanks, Ryn, you're a good partner."

Brad took her hand as he led her back toward the patio, and Ryn felt a thrill of hope. *Allyson doesn't have him all locked up,* she thought. She looked for Allyson in the crowd. Yes, her blond head was still very much in evidence. She was dancing with one of the football players, but her eyes were searching for Brad. Ryn held firmly to his hand.

As he swung her onto the dance floor, Ryn realized there was still one person unaccounted for. She could not see the husky form of Dirk Hudson.

"Where's Dirk?" she asked casually, trying to keep the bitterness out of her voice.

"Oh, him. He's left already. Said he had to get home." Brad laughed. "What an oddball!"

4 · That Dutchman Again

"How was the party, Ryn?" GoGo's voice on the phone sounded eager for news.

"It was neat." Ryn's enthusiasm was genuine. *Most of it really was neat,* she reminded herself. She stretched out full length on the living room rug, prepared to give Go a replay of the entire evening.

"What happened? Who was there?" Ryn could picture Go at the other end of the line, stretching out on the floor, too. Go would expect a complete report—who danced with whom, what they wore, what they ate. Ryn rattled off the details, enjoying her role as social commentator, until she remembered her encounter with Dirk Hudson. She couldn't tell Go about that; it still hurt.

She skipped quickly on to the better parts. "So I danced with Brad three times, whenever he could get out of Allyson's clutches. Honestly, she's a regular boa constrictor."

"Complete with big mouth," Go agreed.

"I can't wait for the campaign next week. I'm going to make campaign buttons for Brad. Want to go to the Mall with me today, while I get some felt and ribbons and stuff?"

"Gee, I'd like to, Ryn, but we've got company coming. I'll help you make the buttons, though. By the way, we missed you at the hospital yesterday afternoon."

The hospital, Ryn thought blankly. The Coral-teens' visit to the pediatrics ward. She had never given it a thought. "Oh, Go," she apologized, "I completely forgot. I didn't have anything to wear to the party, and I had to have my hair fixed and everything. I wonder why Tom didn't even mention it when I played badminton with him."

"Oh, you know Tom," Go groaned. "He wouldn't say anything if you missed your own graduation."

"Did Reverend Carter say anything about my not being there?"

"No, it worked out all right. Some of the other kids couldn't come, either, but there were ten of us there."

Ryn felt an uncomfortable nudge from her conscience. "What did you do?" she asked guiltily. "Did the children enjoy it?"

"They seemed to. We went to every room in the pediatrics ward and gave each of them a game or a toy or something. Then we tried to talk to each one for a while and told them stories and things."

"Was it fun?"

Ryn sensed Go's hesitation. "Well . . . it was . . . it was kind of sad. I mean, seeing some of those poor little tots in big casts and traction and all that. But I'd go again, anytime. It kind of makes you feel good inside when you can make them smile."

The nudge of conscience became a shove. "I'll be there next time; I promise," Ryn vowed.

"Hey, Ryn, do you know Dirk Hudson?"

Ryn felt the hair on her scalp starting to bristle. Why did Go have to drag him into the conversation? "I know who he is," she admitted primly. "Why do you ask?"

"When we were leaving the hospital, he was going in. I wondered what he was doing there."

Ryn swallowed a remark that leaped to her tongue. "I have no idea," she said lightly.

"I think he's a doll," Go crooned.

"Ick!" Ryn retorted. She didn't want to hear another word about Dirk Hudson. "Well, Go, I've got to go work on my dad for the car this afternoon. I'll see you tomorrow."

"Okay. Call me when you're ready to start on the buttons."

Ryn hung up the receiver and struggled to her feet. The mention of Dirk's name had made her feel a little sick. *Get that big ape off your mind,* she told herself.

She hurried to the back of the house, where her parents were enjoying the breeze on the screen porch. Her father was sound asleep, his long form draped the full length of the lounge chair. She stood gazing at him thoughtfully. *That's where you get your long legs, Ryn,* she remarked to herself.

Of course, Ginny was tall, too, with a sort of regal majesty about her. *But no one would ever call me regal,* Ryn decided. Val was pert and petite, like their mother, while gorgeous Vicky was the happy medium. Ryn sighed heavily.

Her father opened one drowsy eye and peered up at her. "Hi, Ryn. What's up?"

"Dad, can I have the car to drive to the Mall today?"

Mr. Drews closed his eyes in thought. "Sorry, honey, I've got to drive down to Miami this afternoon. I can drop you off there if you like, but you'll have to take the bus home. I don't know what time we'll be back."

"That's okay," Ryn agreed. She had long ago discovered that her driver's license did not provide any guarantee for the use of the car. She wandered back to the kitchen, concocted a giant-sized peanut butter sandwich, and dropped into a chair to prepare a shopping list. She had had a sudden inspiration. Those little tiny nails were called "brads." They would be the perfect touch, glued on each campaign button. Let's see—she'd need safety pins, and brads, and glue, and felt markers, and. . . . Her mind raced on ahead of her pencil.

As they headed toward the Mall that afternoon, she found herself humming under her breath.

"You sound pleased with yourself today, kitten," her father remarked.

"That must have been a good party," her mother put in.

"It was okay," Ryndy said noncommittally.

Her father laughed heartily. "Sounds like Vicky," he chuckled. "Remember when Vicky would say, 'It was okay'? That meant she had been the belle of the ball and left twenty broken-hearted boys trying to get her phone number."

Ryndy squirmed uncomfortably. "I didn't mean that," she protested. She subsided into silence until her father pulled up to the entrance to the shopping center.

"Don't feel obliged to buy out the five-and-ten," her mother teased as Ryndy climbed out of the car.

"Oh, Mom." Ryndy made a face. Sometimes her mother's sense of humor was impossible.

"We should be home about nine. Don't stay up all night if we're late."

"Right." Ryndy waved and forced a smile. *Parents!* she thought in despair. *When I'm forty-three, they'll still be treating me like the baby of the family.*

The Mall was a shoppers' paradise. There were forty stores along the sides of a pleasant walkway, with splashing fountains, tropical plants, and art exhibits for added interest, all under one roof. Ryn realized she was humming to herself again as she strolled down the concourse, reveling in the air-conditioned coolness.

Usually she loved to poke through the stores, window-shopping and trying things on, but she resolved today to keep her mind on her business and concentrate on Brad's campaign.

The dime store was a treasure trove. She hovered over the novelties, like a toddler at the candy counter. By the time she reached the checkout, her original shopping list had expanded to include several large sheets of poster board, a package of Styrofoam blocks, and a windup toy that marched in military circles, beating a tiny drum. Ryn could already picture the little soldier with a sign proclaiming, "Brad's your lad," marching across the cafeteria tables.

"How am I ever going to carry all this?" she gasped when the clerk had rung up her purchases. The poster sheets were too big to fit in a bag, and the windup toy soldier too awkward to put in with the other things. "I guess I can manage if you'll tuck the posters under my arm after I pick up the other things," she told the clerk.

Staggering under the load, she headed for the exit. Luckily there were no doors. The store was open to the Mall, but she was already wondering how she was going to maneuver her burden into a bus. She should have insisted that Go come along as a bearer on this safari.

The bus stop was at the far end of the concourse. As usual on a Sunday afternoon, the walkways were crowded, and she found herself apologizing at every step. "Excuse me. . . . Oh, I beg your pardon. . . . So sorry." Halfway down the line of stores, she reached a bottleneck. A crowd had gathered around an artist who was doing a portrait in pastels of a little girl.

Ryndy stopped at the fringes of the crowd, trying to detect an opening through the wall-to-wall people. It looked hopeless. Blindly she began to wedge her way among the bodies, but she could feel the poster paper beginning to slip out from under her arm. She couldn't let go of anything else to make a grab for it.

I'm going to drop the whole mess right here, she thought desperately. And there, directly in front of her, was the husky form of Dirk Hudson.

Ryn stopped short. She couldn't face Dirk. But her stop was too sudden. The man pushing through the crowd behind her rammed into her back with the force of a flying tackle. Ryn felt herself plunging forward, unable to halt her dive into Dirk's midsection.

The bag of nails launched into orbit. The felt markers and construction paper flew in one direction, the Styrofoam blocks in another. Her last glimpse, before she hit the walk, was of the little mechanical man, released from his paper bag, marching cheerfully around Dirk's feet, beating his drum in delight.

She could hear the gasps and exclamations as the artist's audience whirled around to view the spectacle. Humiliated, Ryn lay flat on her face. She could feel a hundred staring eyes. She pressed her forehead against the cement, too mortified to lift her head. There were a few smothered giggles following the sound of Brad's brads dropping like rain over the entire area. Ryndy raised her head enough to see Dirk's shoelaces. *I'll bet he's really enjoying this,* she thought bitterly.

His strong arms were lifting her to her feet. She couldn't look up at his face. As her legs took the weight of her body, a sudden burst of pain shot through her ankle. She winced.

"Are you all right, Ryndy? Are you hurt?" Dirk's voice actually sounded concerned. The big phony.

"I'm fine," she mumbled. She would walk home on a broken leg before she'd give Dirk Hudson any reason to offer her sympathy.

She managed to raise her eyes to survey the scene. It looked like the aftermath of a hurricane, with all her precious campaign supplies scattered like palm fronds. *I want to die right here and now,* she decided silently.

"Here, sit down," Dirk was saying. Why didn't he just leave her alone? If he would just let her stand here and cry for a few minutes, she'd be all right. But he was leading her to a low brick wall around one of the planter boxes. There was no use trying to argue. She had to sit down. Her ankle was really hurting now.

The little mechanical man followed her obediently, and Dirk bent to pick up the little figure. Ryn could see the laughter in his blue eyes as he presented the little man to her. *Go ahead and laugh,* she thought angrily. *Old Tangletoes strikes again.*

"Hey, how about a hand with this stuff?" Dirk shouted to the crowd. He seemed to be having a wonderful time. The crowd was enjoying the whole episode, too. Some of them dropped to their knees and began crawling around among each other's feet, retrieving her collection. Somebody brought out a supply of boxes from the shoe store.

Ryn sat on the edge of the planter, her face the color of the brick, watching helplessly as they filled the boxes with her felt markers, her pins, her construction paper, her Styrofoam blocks, and the brads—dozens and dozens of tiny brads.

She didn't want to cry, but her ankle was starting to swell, and the pain was really intense. Dirk was coming back toward her, and she could feel one big fat tear rolling down her cheek. She brushed it hurriedly away, but he had seen it. His face was suddenly serious. "Does your leg hurt? Can you make it to my car?"

To his car! Dirk Hudson's car? "No," Ryndy protested. "No—I mean, you don't have to bother with me anymore. The bus stop is just over there. I'll be all right."

"You won't be all right." Dirk sounded angry. "You're coming to my car."

"I'm not," Ryn snapped.

Dirk gazed at her steadily for a moment, and then suddenly he smiled. "Then I'll have to carry you."

Ryn pictured Dirk picking her up bodily and lugging her kicking and screaming down the concourse. "I'll walk," she said meekly.

Dirk waved his thanks to the crowd. Ryndy tried to give them a smile, but it came out more like a grimace. Dirk had gathered up the shoe boxes, but she managed to juggle the poster paper and the mechanical man. He was offering her his arm, but if she had to go with him, she was going under her own power. She hobbled determinedly along behind him.

When they reached the entrance, Ryn leaned heavily against a lamppost while Dirk hurried across the parking lot to his car. She realized she was trembling now in reaction. *I wonder if anyone else I know was in that crowd,* she agonized. *Why, of all the people in the whole world, did I have to land on top of Dirk Hudson?*

Dirk pulled his father's sedate old black sedan up to the walk and reached across to open the door for her. She tried to avoid his eyes as she crawled into the front seat. Just because he was giving her a ride, he didn't have to expect any conversation. Her leg was hurting more than ever, but she clamped her mouth shut and clenched her fists.

As they drove along in silence, she couldn't resist glancing across at him. From the corner of her eye she could see that he was smiling. *Great sense of humor,* she thought grimly.

She was surprised when he finally spoke. "I'm sorry I was rude last night at Shannon's."

"I didn't notice," she choked.

"Well, I apologize, anyway."

Ryndy kept her eyes straight ahead. He didn't

need to think that a few words of apology were
going to make up for his bad manners.

He turned the car onto her street and pulled
up in front of the house. He made no move to
help her lift the piles of boxes out of the car.
He sat looking at her with a half smile.

"What's all the stuff for, a party?"

"Election campaign," Ryndy mumbled. She
tugged at the packages. If he wasn't going to help
her, why didn't he just close his mouth and let
her die in peace?

"Are you campaigning for Brad Hamilton?"
Ryndy was surprised at the sharp edge to his
voice. She turned to stare at him. His face looked
strange—closed and tense.

She forgot her anger for a moment. "Yes, I am
working for Brad. Why do you ask?"

"It figures," he said bitterly. He turned away
from her and stared straight through the wind-
shield. Ryn was puzzled. As she unloaded the
last box, he reached across the front seat, slammed
the door, and pulled away with a squeal of tires.

Ryn stood looking after him in astonishment.
"Well, thanks for the ride," she announced to
the coconut palm by the curb.

5 · Too Good to Last

Ryndy yawned contentedly and closed her eyes against the hot sun. The Oliveras' seawall wasn't the most comfortable spot for a nap, but today a bed of nails would have felt like foam. The sky was a deep blue, without even a wisp of a cloud, and a few lazy sea gulls were circling overhead. The world was a beautiful place, and everything in it was perfect.

Ryn had been to the dressmaker's to be measured for her cheerleader's skirt, her sisters had written long letters, bubbling with enthusiasm

over her success, and the "inner circle" at Coral
Cove High had already accepted her as one of
them.

Her campaign buttons had scored a big hit.
She and Go had had to double their original
supply to meet the demand. And her mechanical
man had created quite a stir. Every day Ryn sent
him marching around the cafeteria wearing a
new sign and beating his drum. The kids were
beginning to look forward to lunchtime to see
what message the robot would have for them
that day.

Ryn smiled to herself now, remembering
Brad's words of praise. He assured everyone that
if he won the election, most of the credit had to
go to Ryn. Allyson turned green every time he
said it, but Ryn noticed that she had to join the
crowd and wear one of the buttons, anyway.
Allyson's posters were cute, and Ryn had told
her so, but the compliments apparently hadn't
smoothed Allyson's ruffled pride.

Of course, Brad was a sure winner, with or
without her buttons, but she reveled in his compliments. She had already become a minor
celebrity at school. She could hardly wait for the
elections on Tuesday. They were going to use
Coral County's real voting machines, and the

student council had asked her to serve as one of the poll workers.

It had been a week of almost undiluted joy. Of course, it had been a little nauseating to see Allyson hanging on Brad's arm every minute. Ryn couldn't figure those two. Brad didn't seem to encourage Allyson, but he didn't brush her off, either. *I wish I knew how he really feels about her,* Ryn thought.

She rolled onto her stomach and rested her cheek on her towel. Suddenly a picture popped into her mind of that terrible moment at the Mall when she was lying flat on her face at Dirk Hudson's feet.

She sat up abruptly. She wasn't going to let any thoughts of Dirk spoil this day. With some careful maneuvering and a few artful dodges, she had managed to avoid him in the corridors at school for a week. She certainly wasn't going to think about him now, on a beautiful Saturday morning.

Her only problem today was how soon GoGo would arrive with the boat so they could water-ski. Ryn shaded her eyes against the sun and stared down the canal. Still no sign of Go. Coach must be giving the swim team an extra-long workout today.

Go's schedule revolved around swimming. From November to May, she swam for Coral Cove High, and, from May to November, she swam for the city swim club. As long as Ryn had known Go, she had spent at least an hour or two of every day swimming up and down that pool. But it had paid off. Go was really great. Ryn had not been to many of Go's meets, but she had seen her set a high school record in the 100-yard butterfly at the state championships. *The national record will come next,* Ryn thought confidently. *And maybe someday Go will be an Olympic star. That would be neat—to have your best friend a real celebrity.*

Ryndy lay back on her towel again. Life was funny. Just a few weeks ago she had detested school, and now she was dreading the coming of summer vacation.

Summer had always been the fun time—swimming and water-skiing and loafing around—but now she hoped the summer would pass quickly. The past week had been just an appetizer. She had had a taste of what it was like to be one of the "in" crowd, and she wanted more. But the main course wouldn't be served until September.

The roar of a motor broke into her thoughts, and she struggled up to a sitting position again.

It was Go, in her father's motorboat.

Ryn groped for her gear. Lorrie Schumacher, another of the swimmers, was with Go, and Ryn reached for the line Lorrie tossed to her.

GoGo maneuvered the boat up to the pilings, and Ryn dropped her things aboard. "I thought you two had drowned," she shouted over the roar of the motor.

"That's not funny." Go made an anguished face. "Coach thinks three thousand yards is just a warm-up."

"You wouldn't believe his workouts," Lorrie groaned.

"I wouldn't even believe his rest periods," Ryn agreed. "Do you want me to ski first?"

"Go ahead," GoGo urged. "Lorrie and I need time to recuperate."

Ryn buckled on her float belt. She never felt that she really needed it, even when she was putting her skis on, but Go's father insisted. Mr. Olivera was the original safety-first man.

She threw her skis into the water and jumped in after them. She had thought the plunge into the canal would wake her up, but the water was like warm bath water. Lazily she leaned back, letting the float belt support her while Go and Lorrie attached the towline.

The poor old *Putt-Putt* was showing signs of old age. Go's father had bought the little motorboat years ago, and the whole Olivera family gave it a year-round workout. It was nothing elegant, just a plain old inboard-outboard, but they all loved it.

I wish we lived on a canal, Ryn thought dreamily. The homes along the waterways were so pretty, with the coconut palms leaning out over the water, splashes of color from the hibiscus and bougainvillea bushes, and the trim white boats tied along the seawall.

"Hey, Beautiful Dreamer, while you're floating around down there, your ski is halfway to Miami," Go shouted.

"Oh, my gosh!" Ryn came to with a start. One ski was sailing merrily down the canal. It was already a good thirty yards away. Ryn pulled off the clumsy float belt and took off after the drifting ski. *The tide must be going out,* she thought. The ski was staying just ahead of her no matter how fast she pulled through the water. How did that dumb thing ever drift so far?

She put on a last furious sprint and, gasping for air, finally managed to capture the culprit. She waved triumphantly to Go and Lorrie, but she was really winded. She sidestroked slowly back to the boat, towing the wayward ski behind her.

Lorrie and GoGo were staring at her as she paddled wearily against the current. She grasped the towline and looked up at them. "What's the matter?" she puffed. "You look as though I had just towed in the *Mayflower*."

"Ryn, you should come out for the swim team," Go said earnestly. "I never knew you could swim that fast."

"We need a good freestyler in the worst way," Lorrie urged.

Ryn nearly swallowed a mouthful of water. "You'd have one in the worst way if you got me," she choked. She clutched the towline, still out of breath. "One length of the pool at that speed, and you'd have to bring me a resuscitator."

"But you'd build up endurance with practice." Lorrie sounded like a lawyer pleading a hopeless case.

"You two are serious!" Ryn gasped.

"You bet we are," Go urged.

"Forget it," Ryn assured them. "I don't know the butterfly from the Japanese beetle. Besides, I thought Coach didn't want his swimmers to water-ski."

Lorrie and Go exchanged guilty expressions.

"Well, once in a while doesn't hurt," Go insisted.

Ryn had never understood the reason for the coach's restrictions. She fastened on her float belt again and slid her feet into the rubber shoes of the skis. "What's the matter with skiing, anyway?" she asked.

"Oh, swimming is supposed to stretch your muscles, but skiing tightens them, or something like that," Go explained. "I think Coach sits up nights figuring out all the things we shouldn't do."

"Yeah," Lorrie moaned, "like roller-skating."

"Well, I don't know whether cheerleading stretches them or tightens them, but that's my sport," Ryn assured them. She could just imagine herself trying to keep up with Go in a swimming pool.

Go started the motor, idling it for a moment to warm it up. "Ready?" she called.

Ryn waved her readiness. Go was a good skipper. Some people started the boat too fast and pulled the towline right out of your hands. Others started too slowly, and you couldn't get your balance to get on your feet, but Go had it down to a science.

Go gunned the boat into motion. Ryn felt the tug on her arms and the spray on her face, and she was off. No matter how many times she skied, the thrill was always the same. She loved the sensation of speed, the wind whipping through her hair, the water rushing under her feet.

She cruised along easily at first, simply following the boat. They never executed any fancy maneuvers in the narrow canals. But Go was heading for the Intracoastal Waterway, where there was plenty of room to navigate. If the water wasn't too rough, Ryn decided, she would kick off one ski and slalom on the other.

As Go turned out onto the waterway, Ryn let herself swing wide at the end of the towrope. The waterway was a bit choppy, but Ryn could feel the surge of power as Go accelerated in the more open water. She was in for a real ride today. The wind was whistling in her ears, and the scenery was beginning to blend into a pleasant blur.

Ryn loved to ride the wake. She turned to swing out in a wide arc across the swells made by the boat. The skis hit the water with a slap as she jumped the waves. When she had reached the farthest point in her arc, she turned to swing back again as far as she could in the other direction. Skiing had to be the closest thing to flying—a joyous release from earth.

A large yacht was approaching from the opposite direction, and Ryn looked eagerly at the surging water in its wake. That would give her a good ride. She waved gaily at the young couple lounging on the deck.

But suddenly something was wrong. Ryn could feel the pull of the towline beginning to slacken. The *Putt-Putt* seemed to be out of control. Go and Lorrie had disappeared, and the boat was turning around in a U, veering crazily from side to side.

Suddenly it was heading straight toward her. Ryn tried to swerve aside, but she had lost all her momentum. She was sinking slowly into the water.

Frantically she pulled at her skis, trying to disengage her feet to swim out of the path of horror. The boat was looming over her. Ryn caught one last blinding glimpse of the prow, and then a sledgehammer blow crushed her legs. There was a deafening explosion inside her head. Then there was darkness.

Very faintly, very far away, Ryndy could hear noises. The sounds were hollow, echoing in the distance; she couldn't identify them. Far, far away, and then gradually closer and closer . . .

louder and louder . . . echoing and ringing and clanging until her head was bursting with the sound.

"Make it stop," she whispered in anguish. "Someone make it stop." The roar reached an unbearable peak, and then there was sudden silence. Very slowly, very cautiously, Ryndy opened her eyes.

The room seemed to swim before her. Shapes wavered, taking one form and then another, as though she were seeing them through the mirrors in the fun house. Gradually she began to distinguish white bars on either side of her. *A crib?* she thought foggily.

It must be a hospital bed. But where? And why? Beyond the bars, a white curtain shut out one side of the room, but on the other side she could distinguish a small metal table and beyond that a window.

She tried to focus her eyes on the foreground. Everything was hopelessly blurred. Her legs felt so strange. She stared at them, willing her eyes to see. Thick with bandages, her legs extended upward in front of her. If only they would stay in focus for a moment. Vaguely she realized that a cord ran up from either leg to a bar, through a pulley, and down again. She could make out the shape of weights hanging at the other ends of the ropes.

Traction, she thought dimly. *My legs are in traction.* She frowned, trying to make her mind function. *Traction means something is broken. The weights keep broken bones in place when they're set.*

She closed her eyes. *My legs are broken. Both my legs are broken.* That ought to mean something to her, but she couldn't seem to remember what it was.

What happened? she thought. *Where is everybody?* A soft moan escaped her lips.

"Oh, you're awake."

Ryndy started. She hadn't realized there was someone else in the room. She turned her head sharply toward the sound. A sudden wave of pain surged through her head, and the blurred outlines of the room began to spin crazily. She could feel her stomach churning violently.

She closed her eyes tight, clenching her fists to fight back the nausea. The pain spun dizzily to a climax, then very slowly began to subside. Ryn lay limp against her pillow, drained of her strength.

After a long moment she opened her eyes. Gradually the room began to take shape again.

She realized there must be another bed behind the white curtain. "I'm awake," she said weakly. "Pull the curtain."

The curtain was snatched aside. Ryn turned her head very slowly and carefully to see a girl of eleven or twelve on the other bed. She lay with her head propped on her hand, smiling broadly in greeting.

Ryndy forced a feeble smile. "I guess I hurt my head," she whispered. Weakly she lifted one hand to touch her head. She could feel a heavy swath of bandages.

"You sort of hurt yourself all over," the girl remarked pleasantly.

Ryn's eyes kept trying to close. She forced them to focus on the girl beside her. "How long have I been here? What day is it?"

"They brought you in here last night," the girl answered. "I guess you were in surgery most of yesterday, though. When did you get hurt?"

Ryndy couldn't seem to coordinate her thoughts. Her mind was floating in a vapor. What had happened to her? She frowned, staring at the antiseptic white ceiling over her bed. Vaguely she began to remember. Little pieces of the picture began to come back. She had been water-skiing with Go and Lorrie. She remembered

swinging out into the Intracoastal. And then—
yes—that last terrible moment—Go's boat bearing down on her.

She closed her eyes to shut out the picture.
"What's the matter with me?" she asked weakly.
"Did you hear anyone say?"

"No, nobody said much." Her roommate was
apparently eager to talk. "You were asleep
when they carried you in here. Your mother and
father came in, and they wanted to stay, but the
doctor made them go home. He said you'd be
out for the rest of the night. What's your name?
I'm Kay Randall."

"Ryndy Drews," Ryn whispered. It seemed to
take all her strength to talk. "Why—why are
you here?"

"Oh, they said it's my own fault. I'm a diabetic,
and I went off my diet. Boy, I learned a lesson!"
Kay said soberly.

As Kay talked, Ryndy became aware of men
and women in white moving past the open door.
A young nurse bustled in, her cheerful round
face wreathed in smiles. "So, we decided to wake
up." She beamed at Ryndy. She produced a thermometer and thrust it into Ryn's mouth before
she could ask any of the questions she had ready.

"Wha's w'ong with me?" Ryndy mumbled,

trying to talk around the thermometer.

"Now, you just save your questions for Dr. Quentin," the nurse said with a frown. "I'll tell him you're awake."

She popped a thermometer into Kay's mouth, temporarily stopping the flow of her chatter, and bustled away again. Ryndy lay limp, thinking of a thousand questions to ask but also wanting to sleep again. She was conscious now of pain. Her legs were one constant ache, and her head was beginning to throb.

When the nurse came to take the thermometer, Ryn was too drowsy to ask the questions. She felt herself slipping away into slumber, and then, suddenly, frightening thoughts were chewing at the fringes of her mind. If her legs were broken, would she miss the beginning of cheerleading practice? How long did bones need to heal? Six weeks? Eight weeks?

Ryn realized that the nurse was standing by her bed again. There were so many questions— if only her tongue would respond. "How long will I have to stay here? When can I walk again?" she gasped.

"Dr. Quentin will be here soon," the nurse assured her calmly. Before Ryn could protest, the nurse had given her a shot in the arm.

Ryn felt a blinding frustration. Why didn't someone tell her what had happened? She wasn't a baby. She had to know the truth.

A gentle, motherly woman came in to help her wash up, and a prim, serious young orderly brought her her breakfast, but Ryn barely acknowledged their presence and ate very little. Where was Dr. Quentin?

She lay staring at her legs, deep in despair. She tried to picture herself on the sidelines at a football game, waving a crutch instead of a pompon or leading cheers from a wheelchair.

"Well, young lady, nurse tells me you're anxious to find out what's happened to you."

Ryndy's eyes flew open. "Dr. Quentin!" She swung her head around sharply. The violent surge of pain and nausea swept over her again, and she lay very still, clutching at her covers to steady the room. Slowly the pain began to subside.

The doctor was watching her closely. "Now, to start with, young lady, that is a brain concussion," he told her gently. "You're going to have to treat that poor head with a little more respect for a while."

"But my legs," she pleaded anxiously. "What's happened? How long until I can walk again?"

The doctor took her hand gently. "I'll tell you what, Ryndy. Let's call your mother and dad in while we talk about it."

Ryn held her breath, clinging to his hand while he nodded toward the door. Her parents tiptoed into the room as though the sound of their footsteps might jar her.

Mom hasn't slept all night, Ryn thought, noticing the dark rings under her mother's eyes. *And poor Dad. He hasn't even shaved.* They both bent down and kissed her as though she were made of fragile china and then stood helplessly looking down at her.

Carefully Ryn turned her head back to Dr. Quentin. She tried to read the answer in his face. He was watching her in silence. "How long?" she pleaded.

"Well, Ryn, you have several serious fractures, including a kneecap, which makes things a little bit tricky."

"How long?" she insisted.

"Well, with a little luck, we should have you back on your feet in three or four months."

Ryndy felt her heart stop beating.

"We will have to keep you in traction for a while, but—"

"Three or four months," Ryn echoed numbly.

He couldn't really mean that. That would be into September or October.

Dr. Quentin was still talking, but Ryn didn't attempt to hear what he was saying. The whole world was caving in. It had to be a mistake. Tears she couldn't fight began to well up inside.

She felt the squeeze of Dr. Quentin's hand. "I'll leave you to talk with your parents now, Ryn. I'll look in on you again later."

Ryn stared desperately at his retreating back. Someone had to stop him. He was mixed up. He didn't really mean three or four months. She felt her mother's hand touch her cheek, and she clutched at it as a wrenching sob escaped her.

"Hang on, honey." It was her father's voice now. "It's not the end of the world. We'll help you make up for lost time when it's all over."

Ryndy turned her face away, weeping hopelessly. Make up for lost time? How could anyone make it up to her for missing cheerleading? It was her whole world, the key to her wonderful new life—to Brad's friendship and admiration, to success and popularity, not as Val's sister or Vicky's sister or Ginny's sister, but as Ryndy Drews, cheerleader.

She realized that her mother was talking. "Go-Go's heartbroken, Ryn. She sat in our living room and cried all day yesterday. She wouldn't even go home last night. She said she wasn't going home until we had talked to you, to tell you what happened."

Go, Ryn thought dully. What was her mother saying about Go?

"She says a steering cable broke. There must have been a weak spot or a break in the wire, but it was all encased in plastic. There was no way anyone could tell that it was ready to snap. All at once the steering wheel was just yanked out of Go's hands. The boat jerked around, and she and Lorrie were thrown off their feet. By the time Go could get up to cut off the power, the boat had hit you."

Ryndy listened in silence. One little break in a wire, and it had knocked her world to pieces.

"Go is sick about it," her mother went on. "She's taking all the blame on herself. She's ready to go out and break her own neck to show you how sorry she is."

Ryn tried to smile, a sad smile. Poor Go. "Tell her it's not her fault, Mom. One of us with broken bones is enough." And, in spite of herself, Ryndy felt the tears starting to come again.

6 · Command Performance

Ryndy stared dully at the casts which encased her legs, still strung up by cables toward the ceiling. Had it really been less than two months since her accident? It must be nearer two years.

She couldn't remember a time when she hadn't been lying in this hospital room, imprisoned by those weights and cables as securely as a convict by a ball and chain. Had there ever been a time when her body didn't ache from lying day after day, week after week, in one immovable position?

Had there really been a time when she could

walk and run and, yes, do cartwheels and splits
and tiger jumps? Would there ever be a time
when she would do those things again?

She glanced listlessly at the TV set. Her father
had arranged for her to have her own set, with
remote controls to switch channels and turn it
on and off. But there was nothing to watch now
but the soap operas. She didn't need the trials
and tribulations of the serials to add to the real-
life trials and tribulations of Ryndy Drews.

There was the sound of footsteps in the corridor, and Ryn looked hopefully toward the door.
A visitor? But the footsteps continued past her
room.

It would help to have a roommate again. She
had had a series of partners in and out of the
room during the long months. Kay had left at
the end of that first week and was replaced by a
girl named Margaret, who had a pinched nerve
in her back. They had hung there in traction
together, like two hams in a smokehouse. Margaret was there for almost two weeks. And then
came a girl with a broken collarbone. Ryn
couldn't even remember her name. She had been
there only a few days. Then there was Leslie, who
had been thrown from a horse and had frac-
tured her skull. But Leslie had gone home the

day before. Now the other bed was empty—crisp and antiseptically white, like everything around her.

Ryn couldn't complain about a lack of visitors. Go came faithfully every single day and stayed for at least an hour. They played gin rummy and kept a running score. Ryn had won for the month of June, but it looked as though July were going to be Go's month.

Her mother or dad or both of them came in every night after supper, bearing some treat— special homemade goodies, a magazine, a game, or, best of all, letters from her sisters. Vicky and Ginny had both made special trips home to see her, and Val managed to get away from Y camp at least once a week to visit.

Almost every day one or another of her classmates dropped in. In June, before school was out, Shannon had brought all the cheerleaders to her room for an official meeting. They had elected Meg Garfield captain for the coming year and solemnly pledged that whenever Ryn was ready to come back, a spot would be waiting for her.

But now Ryn wondered if she would ever be going back. Seeing Val, so full of vitality; Vicky, lovelier than ever as a mother; and Ginny, descending from the Olympic heights of atomic research, Ryn felt herself floundering once more in the familiar swamp of inferiority. She was finally convinced. Fate had long ago decided that she was to be the Drews who never quite made it.

A million years ago, in May, she had had a fleeting glimpse of heaven—two weeks of being one of those Drews girls. But you couldn't fight destiny. It just wasn't meant to happen to her.

"Miss Kathryn Drews, I believe."

Ryn gasped and whirled her head toward the door. Brad? Brad Hamilton?

"Come . . . come in," she stammered. Frantically she groped for her mirror. Had she combed her hair since her nap? She must look a mess.

But Brad didn't seem disturbed by her appearance. He inspected the network of cables and pulleys and weights and dropped comfortably into the chair beside her bed. "So you're still hanging around here," he said, smiling.

Ryn tried to keep her tone lighthearted to match his. "I'm practicing a new trapeze act. I could work in a partner if you're interested in summer employment."

"Well, let's see. I've got a cane left over from the time I sprained my ankle, but I've never tried the high-wire routine. I guess you'll have to do a solo." Brad's dark eyes sparkled with anticipation. "Besides, I've got a job for the rest of the summer, maybe permanent."

"What is it?" Ryn could tell that Brad was excited about his work.

"Meet the new disc jockey for WCCF."

"Oh, Brad, that's great!" Ryn was thrilled for him. Brad had the easy manner and perfect voice for radio. "When will you be on?"

"From seven to nine every Sunday night. I'll specialize in records for the high school kids— you know, dedications to the different clubs and outstanding students and all that stuff. On my very first program, I'll play one for you, Ryn."

"How about 'Requiem for a Water Skier'?" Ryn said ruefully. "When do you start?"

"On Sunday next, the pleasant little community of Coral Cove will be treated to the dulcet tones of Mr. Brad Hamilton, Esquire." Brad was trying to make light of his job, but Ryn knew he was bursting with pride.

"I can hardly wait," she bubbled. "I'll have my father get me a radio tomorrow. This dopey TV never has any good music. Gee, I never knew a real disc jockey before."

"I hope I'll be a really good one. I'll sure be trying. But what about you, Ryn? How long are you going to loaf around here in bed?" Under his humor, Brad really sounded concerned.

"Don't I wish I knew." Ryn couldn't conceal the discouragement in her voice. "If I'm not out of these ropes when school starts, I may use one for a necktie party."

"Everyone's anxious to see you back. The cheerleaders are going to start working out in a couple of weeks. Allyson said they have a whole set of new cheers to learn."

Ryndy stared at him, stunned. "Is Allyson going to take my place on the squad?" she choked.

"No . . . no . . . not really." Brad realized he had said the wrong thing. "I mean, she's going to be a regular now, instead of an alternate, but they're still expecting you to be with them just as soon as you can."

Ryn turned her gaze on the two white casts. *As soon as I can,* she thought grimly. *And in the meantime, Allyson Bryant is moving in and taking over, as usual.*

"Well, I guess I better be moving along." Brad stood up apologetically. "Gotta sort through the files down at the station and pick out some goodies for next week."

Ryn knew she had made Brad uncomfortable by her reaction to his announcement, but she couldn't seem to help herself. She tried to force a smile now for his benefit. "Thanks for dropping in, Brad."

"My pleasure." Brad looked relieved to see her smile. "Don't forget WCCF Sunday night."

"I'll be a charter member of your fan club," Ryn promised.

Brad waved and disappeared, and Ryn let the forced smile fade from her face. *Well, what did you expect?* she asked herself dispiritedly. *You didn't think the cheerleaders were going to sit around and weave palm fronds until you were back. They had to start getting ready for September, and Allyson was the first alternate. They promised there would be a place waiting for you.*

But in spite of her own assurances, Ryn felt tears threatening just below the surface. The brave, uncomplaining Pollyanna act was getting more difficult every day. She was tired of smiling and pretending that everything was going to be all right. She let the first tear fall, and the others followed unbidden. She didn't try to stop them. She had held them back too long. She didn't know how long she had lain there sobbing when she realized that a strange, squeaky little voice was calling her name.

"Hey, Ryndy, what's the matter?"

Startled, Ryndy looked up to see the face of a ventriloquist's dummy peering at her around the corner of the door. Hastily she brushed at the tears. "Oh, I'm all right," she mumbled, a bit confused.

"Is there anything I can do?"

Ryndy stared at the funny little wooden face. With his head cocked to one side, he looked genuinely worried. She had to smile through her tears. "I wish there were," she sighed. "Every once in a while I have to go into my 'poor little Ryndy' act."

"Can I come in for a minute?"

Ryn realized with a start that she didn't even know who was behind the door. The little dummy appeared so real that it didn't seem to need a human hand to guide it. "Yes, come in," she managed, curious now. "Oh, Tom, it's you." The lanky frame and long, homely face of Tom Cantrell were a welcome sight. "What are you doing here?"

"The Coralteens are all here today. We've been down the hall telling stories to the little kids. We were saving you for last, like dessert."

"I'm not very sweet today," Ryn confessed. "You should have had me first, instead, like the pickle dish."

"I'll remember that next time. Hey, Ryn"—
Tom's face was suddenly serious—"I want to ask
you something before the others get here." He
sat down beside her bed and leaned forward con-
fidingly. He seemed ready to speak, then was
overcome by shyness. He looked down at the floor
and cleared his throat uncomfortably.

"Oh, I'll ask her," came the dummy's voice.
Ryn smiled up at the little woodenhead. Tom's
lips had not moved.

"All right, Aloysius," Tom mumbled.

"What he wants to know," said the squeaky
little voice, "is about GoGo. I mean, he wonders
if she ever talks about him—like does she ever
mention him or anything?"

Ryn wrinkled her forehead thoughtfully. Tom
was a nice, comfortable sort of person, like a
kindly uncle, but not the kind of boy that girls
talked about or mooned over in their gossip
sessions. "Gosh, Aloysius, I can't remember anything special she has said about him."

Tom sat back dejectedly. When he spoke again,
it was in his own voice. "Do you know, Ryn, we've
been on the swim team together since we were
eight years old, and in Sunday school and Coralteens together for four years, and she still doesn't
even seem to—"

Tom's story was lost in a chorus of hellos from the gang. Ryndy tried to count bodies as they squeezed into the small room. It looked as though the whole club had turned out en masse. Two of the boys were loaded down with puzzle magazines. Go must have told them Ryn had a weakness for anacrostics. Somehow everyone managed to give Ryn a greeting and find a place to stand.

When the magazines had been presented and exclaimed over, Tom got to his feet. "And now, Miss Drews, the Coralteens of the Coral Cove Community Church present a special command performance for Your Majesty. First on the program is Miss Marilyn Armstrong, with an original poem."

Marilyn bustled to the center of the floor like a little girl in a starched dress. She put a finger in her mouth and recited primly,

> "Our Ryndy's very pretty; we love her
> to the core.
> But when she's right side up again,
> we'll love her even more."

Marilyn made a little curtsy and skipped offstage. Ryn laughed with delight and led the applause. Every one of the gang had an act. Go played an amusing song with tissue paper and a comb. Tom did a humorous bit with his dummy, Aloysius, about a girl who broke her leg to get a date with the new math teacher. There were hula dancers and a barbershop quartet and a pantomime.

Ryn laughed at everything with genuine pleasure. They were such a wonderful bunch.

"All right, you characters. It's time to ring down the curtain." The good-natured nurse who pretended to be gruff and ill-tempered was standing in the doorway with her hands on her hips. "There are too many people in this room, you're making too much noise, and visiting hours were over fifteen minutes ago."

Protesting to no avail, the gang gathered up their props and said their good-byes to Ryn. She was still calling out her thanks as the nurse hustled the last visitor out the door and toward the exit.

Ryn lay back on her pillow, still smiling to herself at the corny jokes and off-key songs. The world couldn't really be such an awful place when you had friends like that.

She remembered her words to Go when the group had been planning their first visit to the pediatrics ward. "Do you think those kids really *like* having a bunch of people come in and make a fuss over them?"

She could answer her own question now. *They sure do,* she thought fervently.

7 · Word From the Outside

Ryn edged her wheelchair closer to the window and looked anxiously down toward the parking lot. No sign of GoGo yet. She fidgeted impatiently. If there was one thing that was especially frustrating about hospitals, it was the way time seemed to stand still or move backward. For every ten minutes that passed, only one minute showed on the clock.

There had been plenty of long, difficult days since last June, but today had been the hardest of all. It was the first day of school, the first day of her senior year. Ryn clamped her fingers on the arms of her wheelchair. Everyone else in the whole world was at Coral Cove High today, meeting old friends, catching up on the news of the summer, hunting for their classrooms.

Ryn had lived and relived the school day with them over and over in her mind. She could picture herself getting up early, gulping down a fast breakfast, and rushing out to meet Go—then arriving at school, seeing all the kids again, picking up her schedule, and chattering until it was time for classes to start. And then there was the fun of finding out who your new teachers were, which kids were in your classes, and whether you'd be stuck with late lunch again, so your stomach would make frightening noises all through fifth period.

Then cheerleading practice after school—Ryn had lived through that in her mind, too. The chants and the cheers were still echoing through her brain.

Restlessly she rolled her wheelchair over to the door and peered anxiously down the empty corridor. What was taking Go so long? It was always wait . . . wait . . . wait for something.

She looked down glumly at the two plaster casts. Her legs lay like two chunks of wood, propped helplessly out on the wheelchair in front of her. Ryn was beginning to despise anything white. It seemed as though she had seen nothing else for three months. *It's a wonder I'm not snow-blind,* she thought grimly.

At least there was one consolation in her clumsy casts: She was out of traction. Traction had to be the twentieth-century version of the rack in the old medieval torture chamber. She had tried so hard to keep her spirits up through the long summer—to smile when she wanted to cry, to make jokes when nothing was funny. She had managed pretty well when the family or friends visited, but no one would ever know the gallons of tears she had wept during the lonely nights.

Dr. Quentin would be letting her go home in a few days, but now that school had started, even the thought of going home had lost some of its appeal. Val would be leaving, going back to college, and Ryn's friends wouldn't have time to be dropping in every day.

It would be the puzzle books and the TV, all over again. Maybe she'd surprise herself and everyone else by doing some studying. It would be at least another month before the casts could come off and she could go back to school. If only she could go to sleep for a month and wake up to find herself as good as new.

"Hi, Ryn, how's it going?" GoGo strode through the door.

"Go!" Ryn shouted joyfully. "I've been dying for you to get here. Sit down. Tell me about it, quick. How is everybody? Who did you get?"

Go collapsed onto the straight chair in the corner. "Hold it," she groaned. "Let me recover from my wounds. What a lineup I've got." Go shook her head mournfully. "I got dear old Harkins for physics. You know who I mean. He won World War Two all by himself. And then Davis for world history. There ought to be a law against getting the same teacher twice." Go went on rattling off the list, while Ryndy hung on every word. There was a sort of secondhand thrill in hearing Go tell it, as if Ryn herself were walking the familiar corridors, finding her new locker, sizing up her new teachers.

"Anyone interesting in your classes?" Ryn didn't want to give Go time to pause for breath.

Go rolled her eyes in despair. "Would you believe Allyson Bryant is in three—count 'em— *three* of my classes?"

Ryn felt her muscles stiffen at the mention of Allyson's name, but she smiled sympathetically.

"Now that she's a regular on the cheerleading squad, she's really beyond belief," Go went on. "Honestly, I feel as though I'm supposed to bow my head or curtsy or something when she walks into class."

Ryn knew that feeling. Allyson could put her nose in the air and make you feel as if you had just washed up onto the beach with the seaweed.

Go was chattering on. "And you ought to see Allyson with Brad. Since he started work at her father's radio station, she acts like they were married or something."

Ryn stared at Go, stunned. "Her father's radio station!" she choked. "I didn't know Allyson's father owned WCCF."

"You didn't?" Go frowned at Ryn as if she had just admitted she didn't know her own name and address. "You must be the only one in Coral Cove that didn't know it. Why do you think Brad lets Allyson push him around the way he does? He'd take orders from the tattooed lady if she had an in with a radio station. Honestly, Ryn, sometimes you're awfully naive."

Ryn tried to sort out her thoughts. So Brad's interest in Allyson wasn't entirely romantic. That was encouraging. Maybe he really did like Ryn a little bit. Still, it seemed hard to believe that

Brad would play up to a girl to get a job. He must think Allyson was pretty special on her own. If only there were some way to read his mind and find out how much of his interest was in Allyson and how much in WCCF.

"Hey, Ryn, wake up," Go interrupted her thoughts. "How about a ride in your chariot?"

"Oh, fine." Ryn tried to come back to earth. It would do her good to have a change of scene. She always felt a little like a queen surveying her domain when Go rolled her wheelchair down the corridors of the pediatrics ward. Since she had been unchained from her bed of traction, she had begun to move around and meet a few of her fellow sufferers.

Go pushed her slowly toward the lounge at the end of the hall. There weren't really very many places you could go. Ryn was tempted to tell Go to push her right onto the elevator. She would ride to the ground floor, roll her chair out the front door, and just forget to come back. But GoGo was moving slowly and carefully.

"Hey, there's little Pieter. Let's stop and see him," Ryn urged. Pieter was Ryn's favorite of all the little people on the floor.

There were four little boys in the room, watching a shoot-'em-up on television. The others seemed lively and happy, but Pieter was always so quiet and shy. He was only four years old, with a mop of curly yellow hair that just barely cleared his eyes. Two huge casts encased his legs.

"Hi, Pieter," Ryn said softly. "Remember me? I came in to see you yesterday."

Pieter gazed at her. His wide blue eyes were solemn. "Windy," he said.

GoGo chuckled. "That's right," Ryn agreed. "I'm Ryndy, and this is my friend GoGo."

Pieter turned his serious stare on Go. He frowned. "GoGo?" he asked, puzzled.

"It stands for Gloria," Ryn explained, "but when she swims, she really does go."

"My brother can swim," Pieter said.

"And so will you someday." Ryn could tell by Go's voice that she was touched by the dear little boy.

Pieter looked thoughtfully down at his legs. He shook his head. "No," he said sadly.

"You will; you'll see," Ryn insisted.

"Sorry, girls, time for Pieter's medicine." A starched white figure bustled into the room and signaled the girls to leave.

"I'll be back to see you tomorrow, Pieter." Ryn waved her fingers, trying to smile at the sad little face.

The big blue eyes watched them leave, and Ryn felt a tug at her heart. "Isn't he precious?" she sighed.

"He's a little doll," Go agreed. "What's the matter with him?"

"I heard the nurses saying something about a congenital dislocation of the hip. I'm not sure what that means, but he's been here for an awfully long time. I'd like to just kidnap him and take him home with me."

They had reached the lounge at the end of the hall, and there was no place to go except back to the room. Ryn had a sudden inspiration. She glanced cautiously up and down the corridor. "Hey, Go, do you think anyone would notice if we went down to the gift shop? I'd love to buy something for Pieter."

Go looked alarmed. "Are you supposed to do that? Do you think it's all right?"

"There's one way to find out," Ryn urged. "Come on, let's go."

Go edged the wheelchair up to the elevator doors and surreptitiously pushed the button. If one of the nurses came out into the hall now, they would probably get a real lecture. But the elevator arrived, and the doors opened without their being spotted.

Ryn tried to hunch down in the chair as Go pushed her inside. "This is great," she whispered. "Do you realize this is the first time since June that I've been anywhere except that dopey room and the X-ray labs?"

"If the doctor finds out about it, it will probably be the last time you go anyplace," Go argued.

The elevator stopped, and the doors opened to the lobby. "Look—people!" Ryn exclaimed. She had almost forgotten there was a world outside the pediatrics ward, where people walked around instead of being pushed in chairs. She felt like a country bumpkin in the big city.

Go was panicky. She tried to edge the chair, as unobtrusively as possible, toward the gift shop. As they neared the display window, Ryn caught sight of the assortment of toys and stuffed animals. Pieter would love one of those fuzzy animals.

"Stop a minute, Go. Look at the little pink elephant. Do you think Pieter would like that or the little blue kangaroo?"

But Go was looking anxiously over her shoulder at the people in the lobby. "Huh?" she asked vaguely.

"That elephant—the pink—" Ryn stopped in midsentence. Through the display window she could see a familiar pair of broad shoulders. "Go, we've got to get out of here," she whispered urgently. "Turn this thing around and get to the elevator fast."

"What is it?" Go gasped.

"Turn around," Ryn ordered. "Quick!"

Go was terrified. She almost ran over her own feet trying to turn the clumsy chair around. "Hurry," Ryn choked. "Hurry."

Go moved the chair as quickly as she dared without actually breaking into a run. A few people stopped to stare as they careened back across the lobby. The elevator doors were open, and Ryn clung to the chair as Go shoved her frantically inside. Go pushed the fourth-floor button and collapsed against the wall.

"For goodness' sake, Ryn, what happened? Did you see Dr. Quentin?"

Dr. Quentin! Ryn thought indignantly. She wasn't afraid of Dr. Quentin. "Go," she explained patiently. "That was Dirk Hudson in the gift shop."

"Dirk Hudson!" Now Go was indignant. "Well, so what about Dirk Hudson? I could have killed you, shoving you through the lobby like that."

"Go," Ryn protested through clenched teeth,

"that—that boy—is the most conceited, ill-man-
nered, sarcastic, disagreeable, unpleasant—"

"Okay, okay, I get the message," Go conceded.
"You're trying to tell me that you don't like
Dirk Hudson."

8 · A Setback

Ryndy pushed aside her literature book and stared helplessly at her physics text. There wasn't any use in trying to concentrate on schoolwork. Today was the big day. At two o'clock she would be going to Dr. Quentin's office to have the casts removed—at last.

She had waited so long for this day, and now her mind couldn't accept the fact that it was really here. Was it possible that she was really going to be able to walk again—to go back to school—to begin practicing cheers?

The month at home had been an eternity. After Val left for college, the house seemed so big and empty. It echoed with silence during the school day. And even after school, her friends were so tied up with school activities and homework that she seldom had a visitor. Go still came faithfully every afternoon, even when she could only stay for ten or fifteen minutes, but it seemed the rest of the world had forgotten her.

She hadn't seen Brad since that day he came to the hospital to tell her about his job. She listened to his program every Sunday evening and tried to picture him there at the mike. Several times he had dedicated records to her, but now everything was football, football, football. Not that Brad bragged about his own talents on the field; last week's program had been dedicated entirely to Coral Cove's great Flying Dutchman, Dirk Hudson. It was really sickening.

Ryn gazed out through the open jalousies at the muggy, drizzly October day. She knew she ought to be excited about this afternoon, but somehow she was almost afraid. Last May she had finally been so confident, so sure of herself, but she had had four months to feel that confidence ebbing away.

The judges never should have picked her for

the cheerleading squad in the first place. She wasn't really that good. They had only chosen her as a sort of tribute to her sisters.

Now, stumbling around on wobbly legs, she would just make a spectacle of herself. The other cheerleaders wouldn't really want her back. They'd just feel a sort of obligation because of the promise they had made to her. She should offer to resign and spare them the embarrassment.

Well, at least, when she got back to school, her grades should be fairly decent. The school had assigned her a "Homebound Tutor" to keep her up on her subjects, and he was really a tyrant. He accepted no excuses. Two broken legs don't hurt your brain—that was his theme song. In all her years of school, Ryndy had never been so well prepared.

It was really ironic. Last spring she had worried that her grades would keep her off the squad. And now that there seemed to be no reason to worry about her grades, she was terrified at the thought of trying to lead cheers again.

The front door banged, and Ryn looked around, startled. Who would be banging into the house in the middle of a school day? "Mom?" she called, trying to peer through the room divider into the front hall.

"Yes," her mother answered, "and somebody else."

"Hi, Lazybones!"

"Shannon!" Ryndy exclaimed. "Where did you come from? You're supposed to be away at college."

"Oh, I get around," Shannon laughed. She settled down on the sofa beside Ryn. "It's my mother and dad's twenty-fifth anniversary, so I squeezed out a long weekend at home. I ran into your mom at the store, and she told me that this was your big day." Shannon's blue eyes sparkled. "Aren't you excited, Ryn?"

"Oh, Shannon, I'm scared to death. I feel like a prisoner getting out of jail after twenty years. I won't even know how to live in the outside world anymore."

Shannon smiled. "Oh, Ryn, you'll be fine. I'll give you twenty-four hours to be right back in the thick of things again."

Ryndy tried to force an answering smile, but she could feel a large vacuum inside where her courage should have been. "I—I hope you're right, Shannon, but I look so terrible, and I don't know if I can remember a single cheer, and—and—"

"Now, Ryndy Drews, stop talking like that. It

will all come back to you. You still have all of
basketball season for cheerleading."

"But I—" Ryndy tried to protest, but Shannon
was going on.

"And as for the way you look, that's easy."
Shannon stood up and stepped back, eyeing Ryn
like a sculptor sizing up a block of marble. "Now,
first of all, you're too pale, but a couple of days
out in the sunshine and fresh air will fix that.
And you've put on some weight you don't need.
We can take care of that, too." Shannon marched
to the end table and moved the bowl of potato
chips out of Ryn's reach.

"There's not much to do but study and eat,"
Ryn admitted apologetically.

"Then study," Shannon said firmly.

Ryn watched, fascinated, as Shannon walked
slowly around her, studying her from all angles.
"Your hair," Shannon decided. "We've got to do
something with your hair."

Ryn put her hands up defensively to guard
her two ponytails. "It's hopeless, Shannon. I've
got this blah kind of hair that won't do anything, and. . . ."

She trailed off into openmouthed silence.
Shannon was heading determinedly into the
kitchen. Ryn could hear her voice through the

louvered door. "Mrs. Drews, do you have a pair of scissors?"

Ryn listened anxiously to their hurried whispers. Shannon reappeared, armed with a brush, a comb, scissors, and a hand mirror.

"Hey, Mom, help!" Ryn shouted, but she had to smile at Shannon's determined expression.

Her mother's voice came through the kitchen door. "Go get her, Shannon."

There was no escape. Hypnotized, Ryn watched in the mirror as Shannon threw a towel around her shoulders and began to brandish the scissors. Ryn had been wearing her hair in the two ponytails since sixth grade. She couldn't imagine it any other way.

But Shannon was chopping away like a sheepshearer. The clippings on the towel were beginning to pile up. "Take it easy," Ryn pleaded.

"Hush," Shannon ordered. "You're going to be the prettiest cheerleader on the squad."

"Shannon, you have cracked up completely."

"You think so? Just look at yourself." Shannon pointed triumphantly at the mirror.

Ryn stared at her reflection. Was that Ryndy Drews? The short cut made her eyes look bigger and darker. Her face seemed older, more sophisticated. Her junior-high look was lying on the floor with her ponytails. She felt a nudge of hope.

"I like it, Shannon," she breathed. She stared solemnly into the mirror. There was a question she had to ask—one she had been wanting to ask for a long time. "Shannon, will you answer something truthfully?"

Shannon dropped down comfortably beside her again. "Sure," she agreed.

"When you—when you picked me for the cheerleading squad, was it—was it because of my sister Val?"

Shannon stared at her in astonishment. "Ryndy Drews, you little ninny. I wasn't the only one who picked you. There were fifteen other judges, and I don't think any of them knew your name. They voted by number, and you got more votes than anyone. You're good, you little goon."

Ryndy felt as though someone had thrown open a window and let in the sunlight. She had been picked for herself—not because of her sisters—not because of the family name.

She didn't realize that her mother had come in from the kitchen until she heard her voice. "Shannon, that looks cute. You should be a professional stylist."

"I practice on my roommates at college," Shannon confessed. "They suffer while I learn."

"Well, it looks as though I'm stuck with another glamorous daughter."

"That's life," Shannon agreed. "But I'm leaving orders that she has to lose ten pounds. Pudgy cheerleaders aren't in style this year."

"Not only that, but my uniform won't fit me," Ryn remembered. "So—no more snacks," she promised.

"Well, I better head for home," Shannon announced. "My mother doesn't even know where I am, and I'm supposed to be making the hors d'oeuvres for the party."

"Thanks so much for everything, Shannon." *For more than you'll ever know,* Ryn thought to herself.

"I hope I get to see you with the casts off before I go back to school."

"I hope I remember how to walk," Ryn breathed.

Shannon hugged her affectionately. "You'll remember, Ryn, and you'll hit Coral Cove like a tidal wave. Write and tell me all about it."

"I will, and thanks again."

Ryn could feel her heart beating faster as Shannon disappeared down the front walk. Her life wasn't over at seventeen, after all. She had been a good cheerleader, and she could be again.

And Shannon thought she was pretty. *Dr. Quentin, here I come,* she thought eagerly.

By the time her father got home to take her to the doctor's office, she was almost ready to trundle herself downtown in the wheelchair. Her father seemed to drive so slowly that she wanted to get out and push the car faster.

"How long do you think it will be until I start practicing cheers?" She fidgeted.

"We'll see," her father laughed. "Give Dr. Quentin a chance to get the casts off first."

The slow ride downtown had been agonizing, but the wait in the doctor's office was sheer torture. Ryndy squirmed restlessly in her chair. The other patients, in their assorted casts and slings, looked so patient and long-suffering. She wondered if any of them had had as long an ordeal as she had.

One after another they were called, and they limped and hobbled off down the hall. *Me next, me next,* Ryn thought fervently each time the receptionist stood up to call another victim.

At last the receptionist was calling her name. Ryn clutched at the arms of the chair as her mother led the way and her father pushed her down the long corridor.

"Well, here's my girl. I hear you've got some

casts you want me to get rid of." Dr. Quentin smiled.

"I sure do," Ryndy sighed. "How long will it be till I can cheerlead, Doctor?"

Dr. Quentin laughed uproariously. "Well, let's have a look." He held up a small electric saw. "This vibrating saw won't cut skin—only plaster."

Ryndy watched, fascinated. She was going to see her own legs again.

She couldn't believe her eyes as the casts fell away. Her legs looked like something out of a horror movie. They were a scaly, dingy gray, covered with long black hairs. She looked up at Dr. Quentin in alarm.

He didn't seem concerned. "I know they look terrible, Ryn, but that's not important. Let's see how they feel." He took hold of one leg and bent it gently up and down, flexing her knee.

A stab of pain shot through her whole leg. "Ooooo." She couldn't suppress a moan.

Dr. Quentin's face creased into a frown. "Does that hurt?'" he asked quickly.

Ryn nodded. "It's just forgotten how to move."

But Dr. Quentin looked worried. He flexed the other leg, and Ryndy felt the same sharp pain shooting out from her knee.

"Is something wrong, Doctor?" Ryndy could

hear the concern in her father's voice.

"I was afraid we might have this problem,"
Dr. Quentin said grimly. "I'll need X rays to be
sure. Miss Endicott," he called to his technician.

Ryn was too stunned to ask the questions that
were boiling in her brain. She sat helplessly
silent as the technician wheeled her to the next
room and X-rayed her legs. What had happened?
What was wrong? Why did her knees still hurt?
Why didn't Dr. Quentin let her stand up and
try to walk?

But the prim, starched technician didn't vol-
unteer any information. She pushed Ryn's chair
back to another waiting room and parked her
neatly in a corner. "This will take a few minutes,"
she said briskly.

Ryn slouched dejectedly in her wheelchair.
Her father was pretending to read a magazine,
but her mother didn't even try. Like Ryndy, she
just stared at nothing.

Wait, Ryn thought. *Wait. And wait some
more. And then some more.*

Ten minutes passed. Fifteen. Ryn closed her
eyes and whispered a prayer.

She heard the door open as Dr. Quentin came
in. He wasn't smiling. "Ryndy," he said gently.
"I'm afraid your cheerleading is going to have to

wait again." Ryn held her breath. "A complication has developed here—a condition called osteochondrosis."

Osteo what? Ryn thought frantically.

"It's a fragmentation of the growing centers." Dr. Quentin was trying to break something to her gently. "It sometimes occurs after long immobilization in a cast. There's only one treatment for it—to keep your weight off your legs completely. It's self-limiting."

Keep her weight off her legs? Not walk? Not even stand?

"How—how long?" Ryndy choked.

Dr. Quentin looked pained. "Probably six to eight weeks."

Six to eight weeks! Ryndy felt the world crashing down around her ears again. That would be into December. She stared, unbelieving, at the doctor's face.

But he was still talking. She could hear words like "epiphysis" and "Osgood-Schlatter" and "tibial tubercle." None of it meant anything to her.

She had heard and understood the only important words: six weeks. Six weeks, six months, six years. It didn't make any difference now. She dropped her head into her hands and wept.

9 · Down in the Dumps

Ryndy stared listlessly at the chalkboard as the teacher's voice droned on in the background of her thoughts. Well, she had her old wish—she was back in school. A million years ago, that had seemed the most important thing in the world to her.

She shifted uncomfortably now in her wheelchair. All summer long, through the traction and the casts and the pain, she had pictured the day when she would return to school in triumph, stepping out of her mother's car like a movie star at a big premiere, while throngs of fans cheered and waved. Her big senior year!

What a pipe dream that had been. This morning had been cold reality. Her grand return had created as much excitement as a new grain of sand on the beach. She had lived so long in the dream of cheerleading that she had forgotten that most of the students at Coral Cove High didn't even know her. Some of them vaguely remembered that a girl named Drews had had an accident last spring, and, oh, yes, wasn't she supposed to be a cheerleader? But life went on.

Eight or ten old friends had noticed her arrival and had come over to welcome her and make a fuss over her while dear old GoGo was unfolding her portable wheelchair and her father was lifting her out of the car. But most of the crowd were so busy with their books and their friends that they never even noticed her presence.

Well, what did you expect, a brass band? she thought bitterly. *Who's Ryndy Drews, anyway?*

Mr. Martin, the principal, had given her a hearty greeting and fussed over a schedule that would put all her classes on the ground floor. And the teachers had been pleasant enough, trying to find a place in their classrooms where she could see everything from her wheelchair and trying to bring her up to date on classwork and assignments, but—oh, well—what difference did it make?

This ought to be an important day, but somehow it just didn't matter anymore. All she felt was a numb, hopeless emptiness.

When Dr. Quentin had pronounced her sentence—at least six more weeks off her feet—she had finally surrendered. It didn't do any good to dream or plan for anything. The higher your hopes, the harder the crash when they all toppled down. She had been marked since birth to be the "nothing" child of the family, and she had finally accepted the fact. She had given up. She had stopped caring.

With the diagnosis of osteochondrosis, Dr. Quentin had ordered her back to the hospital for a week of intensive physical therapy. And then it was home again to that lonely, empty house, where the only variations in the lonely, empty day were her daily sessions of bathtub exercises.

For two weeks Ryn had sat in her wheelchair, staring, without seeing or hearing anything. Her mother tried sympathy and scoldings, encouragement and lectures, but Ryn just tuned her out. If you didn't want anything, if you didn't care about anything, you couldn't be disappointed.

Nothing could hurt you then.

Being pretty, being popular, getting good grades—forget it. Failures hurt, but you couldn't fail if you didn't try.

Coming back to school today was certainly not her idea—not like this, in a wheelchair. But her mother had practically pushed her out of the house. "You're not going to sit here and stare at nothing for six more weeks." Well, what did her mother think she was going to do—take up ballet?

"Ryndy, would you like to get a head start to the cafeteria?" Ryndy jumped, startled, as she realized the teacher was talking to her.

"Yes, thank you," she mumbled. She could feel color rushing into her pale cheeks as the whole class turned to look at her.

"I'll help her," Allyson Bryant volunteered.

Great, Ryndy thought. *All I need is a little help from Allyson to complete my day.* But there was no way she could sit there and wait for Go's assistance. Go's class was in the next wing.

Allyson radiated charm, like a latter-day Florence Nightingale. She made a big show of gathering up Ryndy's books and maneuvering her chair out the door. Ryndy could have managed the chair by herself, but it did help to have someone carry her books, even if the someone was Allyson.

"We certainly have missed you, Ryndy." Allyson's voice was all syrupy sugar as they started down the loggia. "Brad talks about you all the time."

Ryn clamped her teeth together. At least her back was to Allyson, so she didn't have to look at that sweet, sweet face. She could picture Allyson's smirk as she talked about "her" Brad.

"You've put on a little too much weight, haven't you?" Allyson was sticking the needles in now.

"I don't get much exercise," Ryndy snapped. Ryn knew she hadn't lost ten pounds as she promised Shannon. Instead, she had put on more. She could imagine the picture they made together —fat old Ryndy and trim, slim Allyson, like the before and after pictures in a magazine.

And, of course, there was Allyson's crowning glory, the long, golden hair falling over her shoulders. Ryn had gone back to tying her hair in the two familiar ponytails. Shannon's haircut was too much bother. It had to be brushed and set every night. Why go to all that trouble, when no one cared how you looked, anyway?

"The cheerleaders are awfully sorry you won't be with them for basketball season." Allyson knew just where the needles hurt the most. "They're such a swell bunch of girls."

Ryndy could feel her breath coming faster. *Why don't you stop?* she thought bitterly. *Why don't you just keep your sweet words to yourself?*

They had reached the cafeteria, and, as Allyson piled their books on the shelves outside, the bell rang to free the others from their classes. The hum of voices became a roar, and the thundering herd stampeded down the loggias.

They hurried into the cafeteria barely in time to avoid being trampled. Ryndy was careful to pick out a low-calorie lunch as Allyson pushed her tray along the counter. Allyson didn't have to know that eating was the only pleasure Ryn had left. After school she could make up for the tiny lunch. Let Allyson think her extra weight was merely lack of exercise.

Allyson pushed her wheelchair up to a table and then brought Ryn's tray to her. *She's so helpful, I don't think I can stand it,* Ryn thought. Then Allyson set her own tray down directly across the table.

"You don't have to sit here with me, Al. Go will be along in a minute. I know you'd rather sit with your own friends."

"Not at all," Allyson insisted. "I'm so glad to

see you back, I wouldn't think of sitting anywhere else."

Ryn felt her stomach churning. She wouldn't
have to pretend to nibble at her lunch today.
She'd be lucky to choke down a lettuce leaf with
Allyson's superior smirk on the opposite side of
the table.

She looked down grimly at her plate. *I hope
Allyson doesn't decide she's going to be Florence
Nightingale every day.*

"Well, look who's here. It must be Ben Hur,
complete with chariot." Ryndy stiffened at the
sound of Brad's voice. Why did her mother make
her come back to school? She didn't want Brad
to see her like this. She could hardly bear to look
up at him.

"Hi" was all she could manage.

Brad collapsed into the chair beside Allyson.
"It's sure great to have you back, Ryn."

"Thanks," she mumbled. How was she going
to live through this lunch period—a big blob
who couldn't carry on a decent conversation.
Where was Go? Why did Brad have to sit here
with them? She wasn't one of his "in" crowd anymore.

But there was no need to worry. In a few
minutes the table had filled with the school's

bigwigs, the "inner circle"—the student council officers, the star athletes, the cheerleaders. They all gave her a big welcome, a slap on the back, or a bright hello and then proceeded to forget she was there.

Ryn stared at her plate and pushed the food around with her fork while they laughed and talked. Her lack of conversation didn't matter in the least. No one would hear her if she did think of something to say.

There was so much they had to talk about— the Halloween dance, a trip to Key West with the football team, and the pep rally. It was nice to have Ryn back again, but there were important things to discuss.

"Hey, Jack, that was a great touchdown pass last week against Miami," Brad called down the table.

"Thanks to Dirk," Jack laughed. "I threw it much too high. He makes any pass look good. I still don't believe the way he pulled it in."

"He's the greatest!"

"Hey, Ryn," Meg, the cheerleader captain, called down to her, "why don't you come sit with us at the next game?"

A bite of apple lodged in Ryn's throat. Sit with the cheerleaders? She might be able to live through not being a cheerleader, but she could never survive watching Allyson Bryant leading cheers in her place.

But Meg wasn't waiting for an answer. She turned back to Brad. "Hey, we better go ask Mr. Martin about decorating the gym for the Halloween dance."

"Oh, you're so right!" Brad exclaimed. He stood up quickly, and the others leaped to their feet, too, as though they were in the presence of royalty. "Let's go," he urged.

They had gathered up their trays and were starting away from the table, when someone finally remembered Ryndy. They all turned to stare at her as though she were some unexpected piece of luggage they had forgotten to pack away.

"Go ahead," Ryn choked. "GoGo's over there. She can get me to my next class."

They all looked relieved. "I'll take your tray back," Brad offered.

"Thanks," Ryn mumbled. She wished that she could just roll under the table and fold herself away like her wheelchair.

The gang disappeared in a clatter of dishes and laughter, but Ryn didn't turn to watch them leave. She had had enough company for one day. She just wanted to be left alone.

But Go had already spotted her and was hurrying across the cafeteria. "Well, aren't you the popular girl today!" Go wasn't trying to be sarcastic. "By the time I got through the lunch line, your table was already filled with the aristocracy."

Ryndy couldn't even dredge up a smile for that remark. "Go, let's get out of here," she pleaded.

Go looked at her questioningly. They had known each other for too many years. Go could read her heart. "Sure, Ryn," she said quickly. "Just let me get rid of my tray."

Ryn waited listlessly, staring at the floor. She wasn't interested in the others in the cafeteria, and they certainly weren't interested in her.

Someone was standing beside her chair before she was aware of him. Wanly she looked up. Dirk Hudson was towering over her. Abruptly she turned her face away, but he seemed determined to speak to her.

"Ryndy. . . ." His voice was hesitant. He must know she detested him. "This is the first time I've seen you to tell you how sorry I was about your accident."

Ryndy kept her face averted. "Thank you," she muttered.

"It was really a tough break for you."

Ryn pressed her lips together in grim silence.

"But I guess you're lucky it wasn't any worse."

"Lucky!" Ryn whirled around to glare at him. "Lucky! You've got a weird idea of luck."

Dirk watched her quietly. "I wasn't trying to be smart," he said. "I just meant there are people who may never walk again."

Ryn was furious. She clenched her teeth and put her chin in the air, looking past him as though he didn't exist.

Suddenly his blue eyes were flashing anger. "Oh, why don't you quit sitting around feeling sorry for yourself?" He turned his back on her and stormed away.

Speechless, Ryn watched his broad shoulders moving toward the door. She realized she was trembling from head to foot. "Quit feeling sorry for myself," she choked. "Sure I will. I'm the luckiest girl in the whole world."

10 · Reluctant Mermaid

Ryndy clung to the gutter of the pool, gasping for breath. The ache in her leg muscles was beyond belief. Was it really worth all this struggle just to prove something to herself and to Dirk Hudson?

She turned around and looked back down the length of the pool. Twenty-five yards. It didn't look so far now, but last Monday, the first time she had tried to swim, she was sure she would drown before she had finished one length. One thing had kept her going—Dirk's voice grating in her ears: "Why don't you quit sitting around feeling sorry for yourself?"

Ryn's temper boiled all over again remembering that day in the cafeteria. Why shouldn't she feel sorry for herself? Who had more reason to be sorry than she did? But she had vowed then to show Dirk that she wasn't just wallowing in self-pity. He could stand around and throw all the nasty remarks he wanted, but he'd have to find some other target.

She had cried herself to sleep that night, but the next day she had called Dr. Quentin. Could she swim? Was it all right for her to kick her legs?

Dr. Quentin was all for it. If she would be careful not to put her feet down on the bottom of the pool, she could swim until she grew fins and gills. At least it would be more interesting than the boring exercises he had prescribed for her legs.

The school pool was directly behind the locker rooms. With a little help from the physical education teachers, Ryn could get herself dressed and out on the pool deck. The pool manager lifted her out of her chair and into the water. Ryn had the pool to herself for a half hour each afternoon before the swim team began their practice. She had tried to do an additional fifty yards every day. Today, her fifth day, she had managed to thrash her way through ten consecutive lengths, 250 yards, without stopping. It was sheer, stubborn willpower that did it. By the time she was half done, her arms and legs felt like chunks of coral rock.

Well, if nothing else, maybe the exercise would help her lose some weight. And it did help to pass the time. Too bad it couldn't turn the clock back six months.

Ryn turned her face up to the warm November sun, anxious to get some color in her pale cheeks. Some of the Coral Cove swimmers were beginning to appear on the pool deck, and Ryn pulled herself up out of the water. They would laugh themselves into hysteria if they saw her clumsy strokes.

"Hi, Ryn. How's it going?" GoGo dropped down to sit beside her on the edge of the pool.

"Hi, Go. I haven't drowned yet, anyway."

Go laughed. "That sounds encouraging."

"How many yards do you all swim in your workouts?" Ryn asked.

"Oh, about two thousand," Go said easily. "Coach will make us do about twice that in January and February, when we start getting ready for our meets."

Ryndy groaned. "Two thousand yards. That's about eighty times up and down this pool."

"You are so right," Go sighed. "I see lane lines in the tub when I take a bath."

"And you don't have a meet until February?" Ryndy shook her head in disbelief.

"March." Go shrugged. "Except the regionals in Atlanta in January. Swimmers are kooky. Do your legs still hurt when you swim?"

"Not like they did the first day. Of course, after I've done a few lengths of the pool, everything hurts."

Go chuckled. "I know what you mean. Oh, oh. Here comes Simon Legree. I better get in there and start picking cotton."

As Coach Helgesen approached, Go slid easily into the water. Ryn hoped her father would be delayed getting away from the office again. She enjoyed watching the team work out.

The pool was built in the shape of a T, with the diving well jutting off the swimming area. There were fifteen girls and about twenty-five boys, faithfully going through their paces in front of Ryn, while two divers performed in the well on the opposite side. The girls all looked the same in identical orange and white suits with white bathing caps, but Ryn could always pick Go out of the crowd. Go's strokes were so smooth and apparently effortless, and she streaked through the water like a wave of light.

Ryn had never been able to figure out the coordination of the butterfly stroke. Go's body seemed to ripple through the water like a porpoise. *I would look more like a seasick whale,* Ryn thought.

She looked up to watch the divers on the far side of the pool. They practiced on their own while Coach was occupied with the swimmers. Curt Taylor, the wiry, muscular boy diver, was testing the spring of the board. He bounced a few times and then went back to begin his approach and execute a high, soaring somersault.

The girl diver, Nancy something, was concentrating on mastering a complicated dive with a series of somersaults and twists. Ryn didn't know much about diving, but she knew that a diver earned a better score if he went high in the air and then came straight down instead of going outward, angling away from the board. But Nancy's dives were making Ryn nervous. Her head seemed to be missing the board by only a fraction of an inch.

The swimmers were working on their flip turns now. Fascinated by the maneuver, Ryn turned toward the end to watch them. She had tried a flip turn once, when she still had legs to push with, but she had lost her sense of direction and ended up pushing off toward the bottom of the pool. *I guess I'm just not the competitive swimming type,* she decided. She couldn't remember a time when she couldn't swim; in her tomboy days she had raced every boy in the neighborhood. But these fancy strokes and racing dives and flip turns were something else.

"Hi, Ryn. Going to join the team?" Curt Taylor, the diver, was coming around the pool.

"Oh, Curt, you're funny! Are you finished already?"

"Ho!" Curt snorted. "We're just getting started. Gotta find out what dives Coach wants us to work on today."

Curt trudged on down the pool deck to the far end, where Coach was organizing the swimmers into waves for the short sprints. Ryndy turned her attention back to Nancy. She was still struggling with that complicated dive from the one-meter board. As Ryn watched, she began a fast approach, took a hard spring, and went high into the air. She jackknifed her legs upward and then reversed into a downward plunge, but something was wrong. Ryn could hear the hard crunch

of bone as Nancy hit the edge of the diving
board. Ryn sat stunned, staring at the water.
Nancy didn't surface.

Suddenly Ryn came to her senses. "Help!" she
screamed, but her voice seemed lost in the open
air and the splashing water. "Help!" She waved
her arms, pointing frantically across the pool
toward Nancy, but the swimmers went doggedly
on, right past her. Coach was lost in conversation with Curt. No one could hear her.

There wasn't time to think. Ryndy shoved
herself from the edge of the pool and took off.
She forgot the ache in her legs and the weariness
in her arms and shoulders. She pulled and kicked
as she had never done in her life before.

Suddenly she was under the diving board. She
could just make out the dark shape of Nancy's
bathing suit far below her on the bottom of the
diving well. Ryn was gasping wildly for breath,
but she grabbed one quick gulp of air and started
down. The pool was fourteen feet deep under the
diving board. Ryn felt her lungs straining. She
was sure they would explode before she could
reach the bottom. The pressure was making a
roaring sound in her ears.

But she was at the bottom. She snatched at the
patch of orange, and her fingers brushed Nancy's

arm. She couldn't hold her breath any longer. She grasped the arm and planted her feet on the bottom of the pool. With all her strength she shoved toward the surface.

It was a long way up. Ryn tried to kick, but the dead weight of Nancy's body was holding her back. *Please, God,* she thought, *help us make it.*

Suddenly her head was above the surface. She gulped in the fresh air in huge swallows. But she had to get Nancy's head out, too. Could she possibly pull her to the edge?

Out of nowhere swimmers were converging on her from all directions. Gratefully she released Nancy into the strong arms of the others and rolled onto her back, gasping for breath. She couldn't get enough of the wonderful fresh air into her lungs. Wearily she backstroked to the edge of the pool and clung to the gutter.

"Ryn, thank heaven you saw her," Go was saying. "Why didn't you yell or something?"

"Yell," Ryndy breathed wearily. "I'll bet they heard me in Palm Beach."

Go stretched out a hand and pulled Ryn up onto the deck. She collapsed on the warm cement.

Coach was shouting instructions to the swimmers who held Nancy. "Easy! Don't pull her!" Carefully they put a Styrofoam surfboard under her and, keeping her body flat and straight, lifted Nancy onto the deck.

Coach dropped quickly to his knees and began breathing into her mouth as the swimmers huddled around them in an anxious circle. Nancy's lips were blue, and her face was a mottled gray. Ryn had never seen anyone look like that. The minutes began to drag on into eternity, and Ryn mumbled a desperate prayer.

"She's breathing," someone shouted. "She's breathing!"

Ryndy managed to lift her head. "Thank you, God," she whispered.

Coach, kneeling beside Nancy, was giving orders now. "GoGo, run and call an ambulance and then call Nancy's parents. Tom, open the big gates to the street. Curt, go get a blanket. The rest of you head for home now, please. No more practice today."

The swimmers groaned a protest. "Please let us stay, Coach. We won't get in the way."

"Nancy's going to be all right," Coach assured them. "She's had a wicked whack on the head, but she's going to be a lot better if she doesn't have thirty people standing over her."

Muttering uneasily, the swimmers moved slowly away, but they lingered at the locker room door. Curt returned with the blanket and Coach wrapped it around Nancy's limp form.

Suddenly Ryn began to tremble. She was just beginning to realize how close they had come to tragedy. Nancy had been very near to death.

The shriek of a siren cut into her thoughts. The ambulance was pulling up outside the fence. Ryn stared anxiously at Nancy. She seemed to be breathing regularly, but she was still unconscious. Ryn understood the significance of the surfboard under Nancy's back. What if her neck was broken?

The ambulance attendants were rushing onto the pool deck with a stretcher. The swimmers pressed forward uneasily as the men lifted Nancy, still flat on the board, onto the stretcher. As they carried her carefully back down the pool deck, Ryn tried to push herself up on one elbow to watch them go. The swimmers were still huddled together in grim silence. The stretcher passed through the gate, but they stood frozen in their places until the wail of the siren broke the spell.

Gradually they began to drift away, coming down the pool deck to pat Ryn on the shoulder or shake her hand. Ryn began to feel cold, and Go hurried to find her a sweat shirt. All she wanted now was for her father to come and take her home. She kept remembering Nancy's body lying on the bottom of the pool.

Suddenly her father was standing at the gate, pale and shaken. "Ryndy, are you all right? I saw the ambulance leaving."

Coach Helgesen hurried over to shake her father's hand. "Your daughter saved a life today, Mr. Drews. She—" Coach stopped, looking at her curiously. "Ryndy, where did you learn to swim like that? I never saw anyone move so fast in my life."

Ryn blushed. "I don't know," she said. "I've been swimming since I was born, I guess, but I didn't know I could go that fast. I was so scared."

"Ryn," Coach studied her face. "Have you ever thought about coming out for the team?"

Ryn was flustered. She hadn't expected this. "I —I don't even know the strokes," she stammered.

"They're not so hard to learn, Ryn. And I need a freestyler. I don't care if you can't do the other strokes well."

"I—I'm not really good enough," Ryn protested. How was she going to get herself out of this?

"You could give it a try." Coach was persistent. "You may be better than you think."

Ryn stared helplessly at the pool deck. She

didn't want to be on the swim team. Why didn't people understand? She just wanted to be left alone. She turned her eyes away from her father. He was nodding his head enthusiastically, urging her to give in.

"Come on, Ryn." Now Go was getting in the act. "You'd be great. What a medley relay team we'd have!"

Ryn didn't know a medley relay from a pole vault, and she wasn't going to let them stampede her into this deal. She shook her head in stubborn silence.

She could hear Coach's sigh as he acknowledged defeat. "I'm really sorry you won't try, Ryn. I'm not just being polite when I say we really need you." He started to turn away, but GoGo caught his arm.

"Coach, would it be all right if Ryn just worked out with us? She wants to exercise, and it would be a lot more fun for her to swim with us than all by herself."

Ryn looked up, startled, ready to protest again. She didn't want a bunch of boys watching her thrash around in the water. What was GoGo trying to do to her? But no one gave her a chance to open her mouth.

Coach was nodding agreement, while her

father and GoGo discussed arrangements for getting her home after practice. No one seemed the least concerned with what she thought of the arrangement.

"It's all settled, Ryn," Go said enthusiastically. "You can start with us tomorow, and—"

"Go, I don't want to practice with the team," Ryn snapped. "I just want people to leave me alone and quit trying to push me into things for my own good. I'm tired of—" Ryn stopped in midsentence. Go was staring at her in bewilderment, her dark eyes shadowed with hurt.

"I'm sorry, Ryn," she murmured. "I didn't realize I was—"

Ryn couldn't stand the hurt in GoGo's face. "I didn't mean you, Go. I just meant—" Go was almost in tears. "Oh, well. I guess it wouldn't hurt to work out with the kids."

Go broke into a sudden grin.

"But if anyone thinks I'm going to swim on the team," Ryn went on angrily, "they're crazy!"

11 · A New Friend

Exhausted, Ryndy stretched out on the pool
deck to watch the swim team finish their practice.
She was as limp as a wet towel. Although she
had been working out with the team for a week,
she still couldn't last through a whole practice
session. Coach Helgesen was a slave driver; the
swimmers barely had time to touch the wall
before he sent them off on another round. Ryn
had managed to struggle through a thousand
yards today, but it certainly seemed more like a
thousand miles.

She didn't even have the energy to hold her head up and watch. She lay on her towel and tried to count the muscles that hurt—her arms, her legs, her shoulders, her ribs—how many muscles did she have, anyway?

How did you ever let GoGo get you into this? she asked herself grimly. *It must be your brain that's out of order, not your legs.*

She closed her eyes against the bright November sun and thought longingly of a giant pizza with a double-thick milk shake beside it. This was really ridiculous. She had hoped the swimming would take off some of her extra weight, but all it seemed to do was to give her an appetite like an elephant's.

What did she care about her weight, anyhow? The "inner circle" had already scratched her name from the social register. She was just part of the school scenery, like the poinciana tree on the patio. Brad remembered to wave as he hurried past her in the corridors, but he hadn't actually stopped to speak to her since that afternoon in the cafeteria on her first day back at school. Allyson, thank goodness, had given up her role as nursemaid and let Marci, one of the girls on the swim team, push Ryn's wheelchair to the lunchroom.

The "inner circle" usually had a table of their own, with Brad and Allyson presiding over the festivities. It was always the gayest, liveliest table in the cafeteria, but Ryn was learning to pretend that it wasn't there. The cheerleaders had not forgotten that she was supposed to be one of them. They went out of their way to speak to her in the halls and in the lunchroom, but they were too involved in their schedule of football games, practices, and pep rallies to spare her more than a passing greeting.

Even Dirk Hudson ignored her now. She made it a point to put her chin in the air whenever she saw him, and he returned the compliment by walking on past her with his eyes straight ahead. That suited Ryndy just fine. If everyone else would just leave her alone, she'd manage very nicely.

GoGo was her only real problem. Go was still suffering from a guilt complex about the accident. She had decided that her sole mission in life was to get Ryndy back into circulation. Go refused to believe that Ryn didn't really want to practice with the swim team, or go to the drugstore with the gang, or meet friends in the library for a homework session, or, most of all, go to see a Coral Cove High football game. Go had appointed herself social director, but Ryn had reached the point where she just wasn't going to be directed anymore.

Here she was, swimming back and forth across this dumb pool for an hour or more every day, just because she couldn't hurt Go's feelings. *Well, I've got feelings, too,* she thought irritably, *and Go will just have to get used to that fact.*

"Hey, Sleeping Beauty, wake up." Ryn opened her eyes to find Go standing over her, still bursting with energy and enthusiasm after twenty-five hundred yards of hard swimming.

"Go away," Ryn said wearily.

"But we've got to hurry. Today's the day we visit the pediatrics ward, and if we don't get going, we—"

"GoGo," Ryn almost shouted in protest, "you are totally insane. I am not going to visit the pediatrics ward today, or any other day, for that matter. Will you please stop trying to save me from myself or whatever it is you think you're doing?"

GoGo's smile faded, and the wounded look came back into her dark eyes. "I—I really wasn't trying to drag you into anything, Ryn. But Nancy's feeling much better, and she's allowed to have company. I remembered how much you said you enjoyed it when the gang came up to visit you, and I thought. . . ."

Ryn closed her eyes and clenched her fists in desperation. How did Go manage to do it—to make her feel like the guilty party? She did not want to see Nancy, and now Go had to remind her that the Coralteens had given her a big boost when she needed it.

She looked up now in angry frustration. "All right, GoGo Olivera," she said grimly. "I owe the club one visit to the hospital, and I'll do it, but I want to make something clear right now. One visit. That is all. I mean, positively and absolutely, *that is all*. And then you are going to let me fade quietly into oblivion. No more social trips, no more hospital visits, no more swim practice. Do you hear me? No more swim practice!"

Go nodded humbly. "I'm sorry, Ryn. I guess I just didn't understand."

"Hey, Ryn, are you riding to the hospital in my car?" Tom Cantrell's lanky form appeared behind Go.

Ryn sighed heavily. Everyone seemed to take it for granted that she was going. "I guess so, Tom. What time are we supposed to be there?"

"Ten minutes ago," Tom said calmly.

"Ten minutes ago? You mean we won't even

have time to go home first?"

Tom grinned sheepishly. "Sorry about that, Ryn. Can't you put your clothes on right over your swimsuit?"

Ryn groaned. If her mother had let her stay out of school until she could walk, and if Dirk Hudson had minded his own business, and if Go had just let her die in peace, she wouldn't be involved in all this.

But her nylon tank suit was already dry. There was really no excuse to get out of the trip. Go brought her school books and clothes from the locker room, and Ryn reluctantly began to pull her dress over her head. "Hey, what about my dad?" she mumbled from inside the folds of material. "He'll be coming for me."

"I'll try to catch him before he leaves the office," Go offered. "I'll call him while Tom gets you down to the car."

Ryn's collapsible wheelchair was no help getting in and out of the pool area. There was no ramp, so someone always had to lift her and the chair up and down the stairs. Tom enlisted the help of some of the other boys, and by the time Ryn and her chair were safely packed into the backseat of the car, Go was rushing down the stairs to join them.

"All set," she gasped, climbing into the front seat beside Tom. "I caught him just as he was heading out the office door."

The rest of the Coralteens were already waiting for them in the parking lot at the hospital. One of the boys had the trunk of his car loaded with the toys and games the club had collected and bought.

They made a weird caravan across the parking lot. Tom pushed Ryn, her wheelchair heaped with packages, at the head of the procession. The others followed, laden with boxes and cartons.

It seemed strange to Ryndy to be returning to the hospital—a visitor, instead of a patient. Even now she felt more at home in these antiseptic corridors than she did in the halls at school.

The nurses on the pediatrics floor were expecting them. They had a list ready for Tom, with the names and ages of the patients. As they stacked their packages by the wall, Tom began to organize the campaign. "Ted, Sue, Betty, and Al, you take four-o-one; Matt, Ann, Marilyn, and Ed, four-o-two; Ryn, GoGo, and I will take four-o-three. Then we'll move on to the next set—four, five, and six. Okay?"

Each team picked out a few toys and disappeared into their assigned rooms. Ryn felt completely inadequate. She had no idea what she was supposed to do. She certainly didn't feel like a ray of sunshine.

Tom wheeled her chair into 403. "Just watch us," he whispered.

There were two little girls, about seven and nine, in this room. Their pale faces lighted up at the sight of visitors. Tom greeted the smaller child and produced a coloring book and crayons. He sat down beside her bed and smiled. "I'm Tom," he said. "Who are you?" For someone who was petrified of big girls, Tom certainly had a way with the little ones.

GoGo had settled down beside the older girl, and they already had their heads together trying to solve a puzzle.

Ryn watched thoughtfully. It seemed simple enough. She should be an old hand at hospital bed visitation by now.

"Hey, Ryn," Tom called. "Come talk to Susie for a minute. I have to go get something."

Ryn managed to dredge up a smile and rolled her chair closer to Susie's bed. By the time Tom returned, she had learned that Susie was almost eight, that she had just had her appendix out, that she missed her family very much—mostly her dog, Poochie—and that she wanted to be a ballerina when she grew up.

"Hi, Susie."

Ryn turned around, surprised by a strange voice in the room. It was Tom's dummy, Aloysius. Tom was really becoming quite professional at throwing his voice without moving his lips. The two little girls applauded with delight. Tom took a seat between the two beds while Aloysius told them an amusing story about his problems in school. He even sang a song for them. Ryndy found herself enjoying the act as much as the children did.

"Well, I'm sorry, Aloysius," Tom interrupted. "We're going to have to leave the girls now. Tell Susie and Jane good-bye."

Aloysius waved to the girls as GoGo pushed Ryn back into the corridor.

"What do you think?" Go asked anxiously. "Ready to try another one?"

Ryn nodded. She could manage.

They moved on to Room 406. Four little boys were in this room. Ryn was startled to see that one of them was Pieter, her little friend from last summer. Had he been here all this time? Almost three months? She signaled to Go to push her over to Pieter's bed. Tom had settled himself and Aloysius between the two little fellows at the far end of the room, while Go went on to the second bed.

Pieter lay staring quietly at the ceiling. "Hi, Pieter," Ryn greeted him. "Remember me—Ryndy?"

Slowly Pieter turned his sober blue eyes on her. He stared at her suspiciously for a moment and then turned back to look at the ceiling again.

Ryndy tried another approach. "I'm still in a wheelchair," she said brightly, "but in a few more weeks I'll be able to walk again."

Pieter made no sign that he heard her.

Ryndy felt her confidence slipping away. "I have something for you," she said uneasily. "Do you like to color?"

Pieter's expression didn't change. Ryn looked anxiously around at GoGo and Tom. They were both happily involved in conversation with their little patients.

A nurse was passing in the corridor, and Ryn waved an SOS. "Is it me, or doesn't Pieter like visitors?" she asked uncomfortably.

The nurse looked down at Pieter sadly. "Poor little guy," she murmured. "He's been here so long that he's just drawn into his shell. His parents both have to work. Ever since his mother had to change shifts, he's been alone most of the day. I think he's made up his mind we're never going to let him go home again. The last few days he wouldn't even talk to his family. I'm sure he thinks everyone is lying to him."

"When can he go home?" Ryn asked.

The nurse frowned. "There's one more operation. It will probably be at least another two months."

"But a month is forever when you're four," Ryn protested.

"I know," the nurse sighed. "Don't be too disappointed if he refuses to notice you."

The nurse left, and Ryn sat staring helplessly at the little blond head. There ought to be some way she could reach him. She glanced back at Tom and Go. Go was helping her little fellow weave a pot holder on a miniature loom, while Tom's Aloysius was entertaining the two youngsters at the other end of the room.

The kids all love Aloysius, Ryn thought hopefully. She remembered that she had been able to talk to Aloysius when her own heart was breaking. That little wooden face seemed to inspire trust.

She had an inspiration. Somewhere in the stack of boxes there had been a hand puppet, a funny little dragon. She rolled her chair out the door

and down the hall. The pile of toys had diminished, and Ryn searched anxiously through the
few remaining packages. It was difficult to reach
down from her chair, and she began to wonder
what would happen if she went crashing over,
chair and all, right into the wall. And then, there
it was, Denny the Dragon.

She tore at the plastic wrappings and pulled
out the little figure. It fitted on her hand like
a glove. She had to smile at the silly face.

She hurried back down the corridor to Pieter's
room and rolled her chair close to his bed. If
there were some way she could conceal herself, it
would be better, but there was nothing to hide
behind.

She stretched her arm out as far as she could so
that the dragon's face was just peeking over the
edge of Pieter's sheet. She lowered her voice to a
deep rumble.

"Hey, Pieter," she said gruffly, "what are you
doing?"

Pieter's big blue eyes turned to identify this
new voice. His eyes widened as he spotted the
face of the dragon.

"I asked you a question," the dragon said
crossly. "Are you going to answer me, or don't
you have any manners?"

"What's manners?" Pieter asked gravely.

"Manners is 'please' and 'thank you' and answering when dragons ask you questions," Ryn growled.

Pieter stared curiously at the little figure. "Are you a dragon?" he asked.

"You bet," Ryn rumbled. "Are you a boy?"

Pieter nodded. "I'm Pieter," he said.

"Well, I'm Denny," the dragon answered. "Haven't you ever met a dragon before?"

Pieter shook his head. "I don't think so."

"Hey, Ryn," Go's voice interrupted. "We have to leave now if we're going to have time to see Nancy."

Ryn threw her a despairing glance. "Just one more minute," she whispered. She couldn't leave until she was sure Pieter would talk to her again.

"You never met a dragon!" she complained gruffly. "I suppose you don't even know what dragons like to eat or play with or anything."

"No," Pieter admitted gravely.

"And I have to leave now," the dragon said crossly. "So I guess you'll never know."

"You could come back and tell me tomorrow," Pieter suggested.

"Yes, I suppose I could," the dragon agreed. "You be a good boy, and I'll try to come back tomorrow and tell you about it."

Pieter nodded. "Will you come back every day?" he pleaded.

Ryn felt a lump come into her throat. Pieter's big blue eyes were fastened on the little dragon's face. She almost forgot to disguise her voice when she answered him. "Would you like me to come every day?" she asked.

Pieter nodded vigorously.

"Then I will," she promised. " 'Bye, Pieter."

She swept the puppet out of sight and wheeled her chair hurriedly back from his bed. Pieter wasn't ready yet to make the connection between the dragon and a human being. He looked at her wheelchair curiously and then turned his gaze on the ceiling again.

Go pushed Ryn's chair out into the corridor, where the others were already repacking the few remaining toys, getting ready to move down the hall to Nancy's room.

"How did it go, Ryn?" Tom asked.

"Okay, I think," Ryn said. She hesitated for a moment, but she had made her decision. "Tom, could you bring me over here again tomorrow after swim practice?"

12 · Swim Like Crazy

Tense with expectation, Ryndy sat teetering on the edge of the pool as GoGo streaked her way through the water. At last Ryn knew what a medley relay was; she was a part of it. Instead of a routine workout today, Coach had been timing his swimmers in various events. "Why don't you try this last one, just for the fun of it, Ryn," he suggested.

Ryn had tried to argue her way out of it. Go had kept her mouth closed as she had promised, but Lorrie had nagged and Marci had coaxed, so here she sat, waiting her turn.

This was the 200-yard medley relay; four swimmers swam fifty yards in turn, each doing a different stroke. Lorrie had led off with the backstroke; then Marci followed, doing the breast-stroke; next came GoGo with the butterfly; and when Go touched the wall, it would be Ryndy's turn to "anchor" the relay with the freestyle.

"Freestyle," Ryn discovered, meant a swimmer could do any stroke he wanted, but since the fastest stroke was the crawl, "freestyle" had come to mean "crawl" to most swimmers.

Go was making her turn at the far end of the pool. Ryn marveled at her speed. When Go's hands touched the wall at Ryn's feet, Ryn could take off.

Of course, Ryn was still operating under the "no weight on the legs" handicap. She couldn't stand on the blocks to get a diving start, and she couldn't flip her turn on the far wall, because that required a hard push with the legs. All she could do was fall into the water and then swim like crazy. *I must be out of my mind even to try this,* she thought anxiously.

Coach had had her try flip turns in the middle of the pool. It felt peculiar to go down and swing your legs around and shove off against nothing but water, but Ryn did feel as though she had the idea. It would be interesting to see what happened when she could actually race toward a wall and shove hard off that good solid tile.

Go was swooping toward her now. Ryn grabbed a mouthful of air, and, as Go's hands slapped against the wall, she plunged forward. It was a good feeling to go all out—to move her arms and legs as fast as they could go. The lane markers were just a blur. She was approaching the far wall. She would have to be careful not to actually push against it. Coming out of her flip, she could feel the tip of one toe barely brush the wall. She had judged pretty well.

She churned back through the water, wondering if she looked too clumsy to the real swimmers. The other three girls were so good that she must look ridiculous by comparison. She came into the finish in a surge of water. "Nice swim, Ryn!" GoGo shouted.

Ryn looked uneasily up at Coach, but he was studying his stopwatch. How could Coach judge the time of a swimmer who couldn't start on a dive or turn with a push? But he was nodding his head approvingly. "Not bad, Ryn." He eyed the stopwatch again. "When are you going to be able to stand up?"

"In about three or four more weeks, I hope," Ryn said.

Coach stroked his chin thoughtfully, and then covered a smile with his hand. "Okay, boys," he called. "Someone give Ryn a ride."

Ryn pulled herself up onto the edge, and two of the boys made a chair with their arms to carry her to the sidelines. After two weeks of working out with the team, Ryn was getting used to being hauled around like a crate of oranges. The boys considered lugging her back and forth as much a part of swim practice as their stroke work.

Ryn craned her neck now to watch the boys swimming their medley relay. Tom was lead-off man today, doing the backstroke. It was exciting to watch, even though they were only racing against the clock.

And you're the girl who wasn't going to come back to swim practice anymore, she reminded herself. *But it's the only way I can get out to see Pieter,* she argued with herself. Her father couldn't take time out from the office to drive her all the way across town every day, but Tom lived out near the hospital. It was no trouble for him to drop her off on his way home from swim practice. And as long as she had to wait around the pool for Tom, she might as well be swimming.

So maybe she *was* beginning to enjoy it a little. Was that a federal offense? *Who are you arguing with?* she thought wryly. *Nobody's complaining.*

Go dropped down on the pool deck beside her. "Hey, you looked okay in that medley, Ryn."

"Did I really?" Ryn was embarrassed at Go's praise.

"Coach is smiling to himself all over the place. I sure wish you were going to be on the team with us."

"GoGo!" Ryn said sharply.

"Okay, okay," Go apologized. "I was wishing out loud. Forget I said it. Are you going to see Pieter again today?"

Ryn nodded enthusiastically. "He's so precious, Go. He tells all his problems to my dragon. Today I'm going to try to get him to talk to me, instead of just to Denny. Funny little kid. He sees me, but he refuses to acknowledge that I'm there. I feel like some kind of phantom."

"Why doesn't his family come to see him?" Go asked.

"I guess they are there every minute they can be, but they're all working to help pay the hospital and doctor bills. His parents can only come early in the morning and then in the late afternoon or after supper. But he gets so lonely and scared. And I know just how he feels."

"If he were mine, I'd just steal him away and take him home," Go insisted.

"Hey, Ryn. Are you ready to leave?" Tom called.

"Oh, gosh, GoGo, will you get my stuff? I didn't realize we were through."

Ryn struggled into her clothes, and the boys carried her through the gate and down the steps to Tom's jalopy. Go waited to say good-bye. "See you tomorrow," she called after them.

Tom seemed to have trouble keeping his mind on the road. "Hey, Ryn, has Go said anything about going to the Christmas dance with anyone?" he asked uncomfortably.

"Tom Cantrell," Ryn scolded. "Why don't you just come right out and ask her to go, instead of beating around the bush?"

Tom's long face reddened. "I don't know," he mumbled. "I just can't seem to say it."

"Why don't you let Aloysius ask her?" Ryn suggested.

Tom's face brightened. "That's an idea!"

He was humming under his breath as he swung the car up to the front entrance to the hospital. Still humming, he set up Ryn's portable wheelchair and lifted her carefully out of the car.

"Can you manage all right, Ryn? Is your father coming to take you home?"

"I'll be fine, Tom, and my dad's picking me up after work, as usual." Ryn smiled up at him. "You're a pretty swell guy, Tom. How could Go help but like you?"

Tom reddened. "You're all right yourself, Ryn."

Tom held the door for her as she wheeled into the lobby, and then he checked her school books at the front desk. Ryn waved good-bye and got herself aboard the familiar elevator to the fourth floor.

Pieter was waiting expectantly for his friend Denny the Dragon. Ryn slipped the little puppet onto her hand and wheeled quietly up to his bed.

"Hi, Pieter."

"Hi, Denny." The big blue eyes lighted in welcome.

"Have you been practicing our dragon language?" Ryn growled.

"Yes," Pieter said eagerly. "Listen. My-grr name-grr is-grr Pieter-grr."

"Very-grr good-grr," Ryn approved. "I think we'll make you an honorary dragon."

"What's ornery?" Pieter asked anxiously.

"That means you're a special friend to dragons," Ryn assured him, "and dragons are special friends to you."

"Oh." Pieter looked relieved.

Ryn decided this was the occasion she had been waiting for. "I brought another special dragon friend with me today," she growled. "Pieter, this is my friend, Ryndy."

Ryndy peeked her own face out from behind the dragon's. "Hi, Pieter."

Pieter eyed her suspiciously, but at least he was really looking at her, not deliberately turning away as he had before.

"She's all right, Pieter," the dragon's voice assured him. "She has trouble with her legs, too."

Pieter studied her with interest now. "You're in a wheelchair," he said in surprise.

"I surely am," Ryn said in her own voice. "I'm not allowed to walk."

"I can't walk, either," said Pieter flatly. "I can't do anything."

"I'm sure there must be some things you can do, Pieter. You know, blind people usually hear very well, and—"

"What's blind?"

"That's when you can't see. What I'm trying to say is that no matter what you can't do, there's sure to be something you can do well."

Pieter watched her suspiciously.

"Like some people aren't very smart, but they're very musical, and some people aren't very pretty, but they have a lot of personality." Ryn stopped. Her philosophical discussion was much too deep for poor little Pieter.

But he was eyeing her curiously. "What can you do?" he asked.

"Well, I can't walk, but I can swim," Ryn answered.

"You can't swim," Pieter said accusingly.

"Oh, yes, I can," Ryn countered. "I'm on the high school swimming team." She stopped then, with a rush of guilt, realizing what she had said. On the swim team? Well, it wasn't really a very big lie. For that matter, it didn't have to be a lie at all.

In spite of herself, Ryn felt her heart beating faster. She had vowed that she wasn't going to care about anything ever again. She wasn't going to try anymore, because she couldn't stand another failure.

But no matter what her vow, she did care. Suddenly she knew she wanted to try again. She would join the swim team. She'd get up and stick out her chin and give the world another chance to knock her down.

Pieter was studying her face in disbelief. "Could I ever be on a swim team?" he asked suspiciously.

"I'll bet you could!" Ryn wanted to scoop Pieter up and hug him. She felt as though she had come back from the dead to rejoin the human race. "I'll bet you'd be a champion swimmer."

"What's a champion?" Pieter asked excitedly.

"That's the guy who's the very best one," Ryn explained.

There was a scraping sound behind her and then the snarl of a familiar voice. "What are you doing here?"

Ryn whirled around to see Dirk Hudson standing in the doorway. "I don't think that's any of your business," she said haughtily.

"I think it is," Dirk snapped. He strode into the room and stood glaring down at her. "It just happens that Pieter is my brother."

Ryn knew her mouth was hanging open, but she couldn't seem to grasp what Dirk was saying. His brother?

"Hi, Dirk. She's my friend," Pieter said excitedly, "because she's a special friend of dragons. And she's on the swimming team, and she can't even walk. And she says I can swim, too," he finished.

Dirk brushed past Ryndy as though she didn't exist. He moved to the head of Pieter's bed and looked down tenderly at the little blond head. Ryndy was surprised to see the gentleness in his cold blue eyes. His voice was husky when he spoke. "Swimming sounds like a great idea, Pieter."

"Denny and I better leave now and let you visit with your brother," Ryn managed. "I'll see you tomorrow, Pieter." She whisked her chair out the door, not sure that Pieter had even heard her good-bye.

Sometimes you are really stupid, Kathryn, she told herself. *You should have made the connection—the blue eyes, the blond hair, Dirk in the gift shop.*

She pushed the button for the self-service elevator. Her father wouldn't be here for another twenty minutes or so. She would have to hide down in the lobby.

Now I know why Dirk said I was lucky—that there were people who might never walk again. Ryn felt a hot blush of shame. As bad as her accident had been, it was nothing compared to poor little Pieter's suffering.

Then she remembered Dirk's snarl at finding her with Pieter. *But he's still an insufferable, supercilious boor,* she thought angrily. The elevator doors opened and Ryn fled down to the lobby.

13 · A Night of Discovery

Still a little unsteady on her feet, Ryn climbed out of Tom's car and stood uncertainly on the sidewalk in front of the school. It was going to take her a few more days to get the feel of walking again. Her legs didn't seem to belong to her at all.

Go squeezed her arm excitedly. "Ryn and I will wait on the bench while you park, Tom."

Ryn leaned on Go as they made their way down the gaily lighted walkway toward the entrance of Coral Cove High. The big night had

come. Tom had finally worked up enough nerve
to ask Go to the Christmas formal. Aloysius
had asked her in Tom's behalf, like a little
wooden John Alden. And now, here was Ryn,
intruding on their date like a chaperon.

"Go, I really feel like a rat, butting in on your
date," she apologized.

"Ryndy Drews," Go scolded, "you didn't butt
in; we invited you. Tom and I both would have
been disappointed if you hadn't come. I can't
wait to see the kids' faces when you walk in the
door under your own steam."

They had reached the little concrete bench,
and Ryndy sank down gratefully. Her vanity had
persuaded her to leave her crutches at home
tonight, but she realized now that her vanity
wasn't going to hold her up if her legs gave way.
She wouldn't attempt to do any dancing tonight,
but it would be fun to watch the others and listen
to the music. Go looked so pretty. In spite of her
sturdy, athletic build, the sparkling silver party
dress made her look almost delicate.

Ryn hoped her own pale blue chiffon wasn't
too baggy. It had been new last spring, but she
had never had a chance to wear it. Six weeks of
working out with the team had really slimmed
her down. She was much trimmer now than on

the day she broke her legs.

Tom appeared out of the darkness. "Okay, ladies, here we go." He took a girl on each arm as they entered the main gate.

The patio, as well as the cafeteria, had been decorated for the occasion. It was a little incongruous to have an artificial snowman standing under the palm trees, with make-believe icicles dangling through the hibiscus blossoms, but no one seemed to mind.

The music of the band grew deafening as they stepped into the crowded cafeteria, but Ryn could hear the squeals of delight and surprise as one by one the dancers and the bystanders realized that she was walking in on her own two feet. She was surrounded by an excited crowd of well-wishers.

"Ryn, you're walking!" "How does it feel?" "Can you dance?" "Hey, this is great." She was embarrassed by all the attention.

She caught sight of Brad Hamilton waving to her from across the room. "Save a dance for me, Ryn," he shouted.

She smiled and shook her head, pointing at her wobbly legs.

The tables had been arranged in a horseshoe facing the lively band. They found a table that offered a good view of the entire scene. Tom helped Ryn into a chair and Go settled down beside her.

"I'll go get us some punch," Tom offered.

Ryn sat back to marvel at the appearance of the cafeteria. It was amazing what a little crepe paper and tinsel could do. It was hard to believe that this festive hall was the plain old lunchroom she sat in every day.

Tom reappeared with the punch, and the three of them offered a series of toasts. "To Tom, the captain of the greatest swim team in South Florida." A gulp of punch.

"To GoGo, state champ and future Olympic flyer." Another gulp.

"To Ryn, the girl with the walkable legs and our great new sprinter." Another gulp and then a burst of laughter as Tom pretended to be drowning in his punch.

"Hey, Go, did you tell Ryn about the big Christmas meet?"

Ryn looked up in surprise. Maybe she wasn't hearing correctly over the sound of the band. "Christmas? I thought we weren't supposed to have a meet until March!"

"It's something new," Tom explained. "Some of the high school coaches didn't like the idea of taking their swimmers up to the regionals in Atlanta before they'd had a single meet at home. So the Gold Coast counties are going to have a special meet during Christmas vacation. The coaches can enter anyone they're planning to take to Atlanta."

Ryn stared, wide-eyed. "Regionals in Atlanta?" she asked.

"Oh, that's not till late in January," Go assured her. "The whole team doesn't go. Just the swimmers who can meet the qualifying times."

Ryn relaxed. "Well, that's not me," she said in relief.

"Yes, it is," Tom put in. "Coach wants to send your medley relay team to Atlanta—you and Go and Lorrie and Marci. He's entered the relay in the Christmas meet, so you'll have a chance for a little experience, Ryn."

Ryn heard her ice clinking in her glass as her hand trembled. "Where—where's it going to be?"

"At the Swimming Hall of Fame pool in Fort Lauderdale."

"But I thought they always had the College Coaches' Swim Forum there during Christmas vacation, with all those college swimmers and national champions and everything."

"They do, and all kinds of other events, like a

water show and a big international meet, and they induct famous swimmers into the Hall of Fame and all that. But they'll just be starting to arrive when we have our meet."

"You don't think any of them will be there to watch us swim, do you?" Ryn asked with concern. She couldn't imagine diving into a pool in front of a crowd of celebrities and swimmers from all over the country.

"Not a chance," Tom assured her.

Ryn stared weakly at the angel on top of the huge Christmas tree. She'd thought she had three months to get up her courage for her first meet, but Christmas vacation—why, that was only a few weeks away!

Suddenly the table was surrounded by a new group of well-wishers. Nancy, the diver, and Meg, the captain of the cheerleaders, were in the crowd.

"Ryn, it's so great to see you walking." Nancy beamed. "How are you feeling?"

"The question is how are *you* feeling, Nan?" Ryn asked eagerly.

"Oh, I'm fine." Nancy smiled. "Almost as good as new. The doctor says I can start diving again after Christmas."

"That's wonderful! I know how you must feel.

I can hardly wait to try swimming, now that I can stand on the blocks and do a real flip turn off the wall."

Nancy hugged her shoulders. "Well, I thank the good Lord every day that you could swim at all with those legs of yours, Ryn."

Ryn blushed with pleasure.

"I sure wish you could have led cheers without them," Meg put in. "We've missed having you on the squad."

"Not as much as I missed being there," Ryn assured her.

"I didn't see you at any of the football games." Meg frowned. "I thought you were going to come out and sit with us."

Ryn avoided Meg's eyes. Meg didn't have to know her real reasons for staying away. "It was a little complicated trying to get there in a wheel-chair," she mumbled.

"We really had a great team this year. Dirk Hudson is so fabulous; you wouldn't believe it."

Dirk again, Ryn thought. *You'd think he was the only one on the team.* She forced a smile. "I heard he was pretty fantastic."

"He's sure to be All-State halfback," Meg enthused. "Well, we better get going and refill the punch bowl."

The group moved on with a chorus of congratulations. The dance floor was crowded now,
and Tom was tapping his fingers in time to the
music. Ryn didn't want Tom and Go to feel they
had to spend the evening keeping her company.
"You two go ahead and dance," she urged. "I
won't be lonely."

It took a little persuasion, but they finally gave
in and joined the dancers. Colored spotlights
were sweeping the floor, and Ryn tried to pick
faces out of the crowd. She spotted Brad, dancing
cheek to cheek with—no, it wasn't Allyson. It
was another girl, an unfamiliar face. Ryn was
sure she had never before seen that flaming red
hair at Coral Cove.

"Hi, Ryn, how are you?" Ryndy was surprised
to see Allyson sliding into the chair beside her.

"I'm a little wobbly, but I feel wonderful,"
Ryn replied with a smile.

"I'm really glad you're walking again," Allyson said earnestly.

Ryn studied her face. Allyson's usual haughty
smirk was missing. She looked almost forlorn, in
spite of her elaborate hairdo and expensive dress.
"Thanks," Ryn murmured.

She could see that Allyson's mind was on the
dance floor with Brad and his unfamiliar partner.

She decided to dive in headfirst. "Who's that with Brad? I've never seen her before."

Allyson's face tightened, but she tried to make her voice sound gay and unconcerned. "Oh, her name is Sharon something. She's Buddy's cousin, here from New York." A trace of bitterness crept into Allyson's voice. "Her brother-in-law is a big TV producer or something."

Allyson trailed off into silence, but she didn't need to say anything more. Ryn got the picture. The daughter of a radio station owner was a nice catch, but the sister-in-law of a TV producer was even better. Ryn was surprised to find herself actually feeling sorry for Allyson.

Brad could really make a girl feel as though she were the big event in his life. But watch out when he decided that another lawn was a little bit greener. Brad would put Allyson away with the other trophies on his shelf, while he worked his way up to the next prize.

The music ended, and the dancers started to move off the floor. Allyson got to her feet hurriedly, almost knocking her chair down in her haste. "Oh, excuse me, Ryn. I've got to run. I'll see you later."

Ryn watched her hurry down the hall to intercept Brad as he left the dance floor. *Good luck,* she thought sympathetically.

Tom and Go joined her again as the band took an intermission. The room seemed full to the bursting point, and the laughter and chatter were almost as loud as the music had been.

"Hey, Ryn, look who's coming!" Go pointed across the room.

"Oh, no," Ryndy groaned. "Not Dirk." He was obviously heading for their table. She was trapped.

Dirk didn't bother with formalities like "Hello" or "How are you?" He came right to the point. "Ryn, I want to talk to you."

Ryn tried to appear aloof. She pointed to the empty chair beside her.

"No, alone," he said intently.

"We'll leave," Tom offered, starting to get up.

"No," Dirk shook his head. "Will you come out on the patio for a few minutes, Ryn?"

She stared at him indignantly. Who did he think he was, forever barging into her life, insulting her, ordering her around? But he looked so serious that she felt a wave of alarm. Maybe something had happened to Pieter.

"All right," she agreed uneasily. She rose unsteadily to her feet. Dirk offered her his arm, and, although she would have preferred to march proudly down the hall independently, she had to admit it was good to have something strong to lean on.

As they crossed the dance floor, Brad suddenly appeared in front of them. "Hey, Ryn, are you ready for that dance you promised?"

Dirk almost yanked her off her feet to pull her around Brad. "She's with me," he said.

Outraged, Ryn glared up at Dirk. *There he goes again,* she fumed to herself. *I don't care if I ever see Brad Hamilton again, but I'm perfectly capable of telling him so myself.*

But Dirk was pulling her on toward the door, his face set in grim lines. Ryn was swept resentfully along beside him.

The air on the patio was cool, and Ryn shivered a little as they stepped out into the night. Couples were sitting at the little round cement tables or standing in the shadows.

Dirk led her to a small bench in the corner, away from the others. He waited until she was seated and then stood by, looking down at her intently.

It is Pieter. I know something's happened, she thought anxiously. But when Dirk spoke, his voice was soft. "Ryn, I've been every kind of a darn fool. I owe you so many apologies, I don't even know where to start."

Ryn stared at him in surprise.

"I'm just beginning to realize what you've done for Pieter. We were so worried about him. He was getting more and more depressed and withdrawn. Nothing we did or said seemed to shake him out of it. And then all at once, a few weeks ago, he began to perk up. I didn't know why, but I was so happy about it, I didn't even care. And then the nurse told me today about your little dragon. You've been going in to see him every day!"

Ryn nodded, embarrassed at Dirk's words.

"Ryn, you probably saved his sanity. Mom and Dad have been working day and night trying to earn the money for the doctors and the hospital bills. I wanted to get a job, too, afternoons after school, like my sister Katrina, but my dad said I had to stay on the football team. It was my best chance for a college scholarship, and I had to have one. I stuck it out with the team, and I guess it's going to pay off, but those last few weeks were almost too much for Pieter—until you came along."

Ryn couldn't meet his eyes. She felt guilty that she hadn't gone to see Dirk play a single game all season.

"Anyway, Ryn, you've got to let me explain a few things. You remember that first night you came out on the dock at Shannon's house?"

Did she remember? Even now Ryn felt a wave of humiliation, just thinking of it.

"We had expected that Pieter would be coming home. Then that evening, when I went to the hospital to see him, I found out he needed still another operation. I was sick. I should never have gone to the party at all, but I didn't know what to do with myself. And then you came out on the dock, and you sounded so—so cheerful, and—well, there's still no excuse for my being so rude."

Ryndy hung her head. *Me and my phony "Val manner,"* she thought.

"And then that day I brought you home from the Mall. . . . Ryn, I don't like to cut people up behind their backs, but I guess I should have explained, instead of just slamming off and leaving you standing there on the curb. You see, I've seen Brad operate before. My sister Kat is a part-time typist at WCCF. Brad was giving her a big rush, until he found out Allyson's father owned the station. And then—wham! Good-bye, Kat; hello, Allyson. When you told me you were buying all that stuff to make Brad's campaign buttons—well, I just hated to see him make a fool out of you, too."

"I fell for his line," she admitted. "It took me a while, but I think I understand dear Brad now."

"I'm glad of that." Dirk almost smiled. "And then that day in the cafeteria. It was Pieter again. I had been in to see him the night before, and he wouldn't even talk to me. He hardly seemed to know I was there. I was half crazy with worry, but I had no right to talk to you like that."

"You did me a favor," Ryn said quietly. "I really was feeling sorry for myself. I needed a good swift kick."

"But who was I to say that to you? If I had been through what you had, I'd have cracked up, for sure."

"But I started swimming then, just to show you you were wrong about me, and it was the best thing I ever did."

Dirk sat down beside her and looked at her eagerly. "Pieter says you told him he could swim. Do you really think he could?"

Ryn caught his excitement. "I'm sure he could," she said eagerly. "He wouldn't have to use his legs."

"He'll be coming home soon. Will you help me teach him?"

"I'd love to," Ryn breathed. "He's such a dear little guy."

Dirk was watching her now, thoughtfully. "You know, you're not at all like I thought you were," he whispered. "I thought all you cared about was being one of the 'inner circle,' a big shot cheerleader running around with the wheels and all that."

Ryn smiled. "I had a bad case of big-sisteritis. You don't know what it was like to follow those three into Coral Cove High. I knew I could never be a brain like Ginny or a raving beauty like Vicky, so I figured my only chance to count in the family at all was to be a cheerleader like Val."

Dirk was listening to her, waiting for her to go on. Ryn hadn't intended to tell her life story, but he seemed to want to hear it.

"But maybe you were right about me. I guess I wanted to be a cheerleader because—well, because it's glamorous—because you're sort of automatically 'in.' I didn't really care that much about cheerleading. But the swimming is different. It's funny: I started it to spite you, and then I stuck with it just to get a ride to the hospital to see Pieter, and now—" Ryn paused— "now I want to be a good swimmer. Not to impress anyone, because I'll never be a champ like GoGo, but just because—well, it's a challenge. My sisters always tried to do everything for me, to give me life on a silver platter. But no one can give you swimming. You have to fight for every second, all by yourself."

Ryn stopped, but Dirk was still watching her face. "I didn't mean to make a speech," she apologized.

Dirk took her hand and held it in both of his. "I don't know your sisters," he said quietly, "but they couldn't begin to measure up to you."

Ryn looked into the deep blue eyes. Had she once thought that Dirk Hudson was smug and selfish and arrogant? All she could see now were the strength and the tenderness in his face.

"You're not at all like I thought you were," she breathed.

14 · Unknown Factor

Ryndy stared around like a rubberneck tourist. They were actually in Fort Lauderdale, at the beautiful Swimming Hall of Fame. She felt as though she were treading on hallowed ground. With Tom and Go she had walked to the end of the small projection of land which jutted out into the Intracoastal Waterway, passing the huge Olympic-sized pool to stand beside the lovely Hall of Fame building. On one side was Bahia Mar, the big marina where luxurious yachts were docked, row after row. On the other side, up the waterway, was the graceful sweep of the Las Olas bridge. Ryn stood motionless, trying to take in the entire scene: the dramatic lines of the building, the beautiful landscaping, and, across the waterway, the fabulous homes with graceful palms.

"Ryn, look at this." GoGo tugged at her arm. In the curve of the circular drive were squares of cement with the handprints and footprints of the aquatic greats. Ryn picked out names like Johnny Weissmuller, Buster Crabbe, and Esther Williams.

What am I doing here? she thought weakly.

"Hey, come on, you two," Tom called. "The rest of the gang are already inside. You won't even have time to warm up."

They hurried back down the driveway and up several steps to the long concourse that ran across the entire front of the pool complex. The pool was hidden from their view by large green panes of Plexiglas, which served to break the wind coming off the ocean. Ryn turned to look back across the narrow strip of land, trying to catch a glimpse of the blue Atlantic, frosted with whitecaps on this windy December day. She felt as though she were on a movie set.

Tom was urging them on. "Come on, they're

getting ready to start. Let's warm up."

Ryn and Go hurried through the gate, and Ryn found herself gaping again. She had never seen such a big pool. Beyond the pool was a separate diving well, with the high diving tower etched against the sky.

She stared again at the long expanse of water, which seemed to stretch out forever. "It's so big," she gasped.

Go looked at her in surprise. "Haven't you ever seen a fifty-meter pool before?"

Ryn shook her head weakly. "I thought Coral Cove High pool was big," she murmured.

The pool deck was jammed with coaches and swimmers and officials. "There's Coach with the kids." Tom pointed to a small group in orange jackets gathering at the far end of the pool deck. As they made their way through the crowd, Ryn stared openly at the other swimmers. The vari-colored jackets and sweat shirts bore names like Miami, Hollywood, Palm Beach, Hialeah. *Every high school swimmer in South Florida must be here,* she worried silently.

The Coral Cove swimmers were clustered around Coach Helgesen. "Get in the water and loosen up," Coach was shouting. "You can warm up in the diving well when the meet starts, but the medley relay is the first event."

"The first event!" Ryn choked. Her stomach did a double somersault with a half twist.

"The medley relay always comes first," Go explained. "All the school meets have the same order of events."

Ryn looked around at the others. They all seemed so at ease and relaxed. *I'm the only one on the whole team who has never been in a meet before,* she thought, more worried than ever.

"Let's get in the water, Ryn," Go urged.

Ryn pulled off her jacket and moved slowly to the edge of the pool. She took one last anxious glance up at the stands. Spectators were beginning to file in, but there was no sign yet of a certain blond head. The swim team had come to Fort Lauderdale with Coach on the bus, but her parents were driving down by car. Dirk had promised to come with them.

I hope they know the relay is first, she worried. Ever since the Christmas formal, Dirk had become a part of her life. He waited for her to finish practice every day, and then they went to the hospital to see Pieter. There was no money for dates, but they spent their weekends listening to Ryn's records or walking on the beach. Ryn couldn't imagine swimming without Dirk there.

But GoGo was already in the water, and Ryn plunged in after her. The heated pool was comfortably warm, and she felt her tense muscles beginning to loosen and stretch as she pulled through the water.

She was relieved to notice that the lane markers were laid out across the width of the pool instead of the length. They would be swimming twenty-five yard widths, just as they did in their own pool at Coral Cove. Ryn had never tried to swim fifty meters straight out, without a turn.

A shrill whistle sounded, and a voice came over the loudspeaker. "Swimmers, clear the pool."

Ryn swam hastily to the edge and pulled herself out as the loudspeaker continued. "Will you please stand for the national anthem."

She pulled her jacket around her shoulders and stood at attention. Her head was high, but her heart was pounding as the flag was raised. She was trembling, but she wasn't sure if it was the excitement, the cold, or just plain fright.

"Please remain standing for the invocation."

Ryndy started to bow her head, when she caught a glimpse of a pair of broad shoulders in the stands. She craned her neck eagerly. Yes, they were here, Dirk, her mother and father, and—

and Val. Her sister Val was here, too!

For a moment the old inferiority feelings engulfed her. What if she goofed the whole thing up, with all of them watching her? What if she jumped the start and went into the water before Go touched the wall? Their relay team would be disqualified. No, she wouldn't even think about such a thing.

Her family had seen her now, and she waved, trying to put on a bright smile. Val gave her an excited wave, and Dirk clasped his hands over his head in a victory gesture.

The loudspeaker shrieked again. "Will the first heat of the girls' medley relay report to the clerk of the course."

Ryn looked anxiously at Go. "Is that us?"

Go shook her head. "No, we're seeded in the last heat."

Ryn hated to display her ignorance, but she had to ask. "What does that mean?"

"Well, usually in a big meet, they have preliminaries in the morning and finals at night. All the teams swim in the preliminary heats, and then the six fastest teams come back and swim off against each other in the finals. When they have finals at night, they mix the fast teams in among the slow ones in the morning.

"But this is what they call a timed final. Every team swims, and they just pick the winners by the fastest times. They'll put all the fastest teams in the last heat together so that they'll push each other harder. The fastest is in Lane Three, next fastest in Lane Four, then Two, Five, One, and Six. We're seeded third, in Lane Two."

"But how do they know who's fastest, when we haven't even been in a meet?" Ryn asked.

"The coaches have to estimate a time for their teams, according to what they've done so far in practice."

"Are we really supposed to be one of the fastest?" Ryn asked innocently.

Tom broke in laughing. "We hope so. We'll soon know."

Ryn watched uneasily as the backstrokers of the first heat took their positions in the water. The announcer was already calling for the second heat to report.

I'm the unknown factor, she told herself. *I'm Miss X. GoGo holds the state record in the fly, and Lorrie won the Coral County championships in the backstroke last year.* Marci was a bit of a question mark in the breaststroke. She had just moved down from the north, but her times there had been good. Ryn was the only one who had

THE FAMILY NAME   201

never swum in competition.

And the competition was rough on the Florida
Gold Coast. Most of these swimmers had been
working out the year around, on city or club
teams, since they were babies.

The gun went off, and the first heat was under
way. Ryn couldn't believe her eyes. If this was
the slow heat, she didn't want to see the fast
ones. Her only chance was that the other three
girls could build up such a big lead that she
couldn't possibly ruin it for them. The first heat
finished in a wild surge of water, and the second
heat began to take their positions.

"Third heat of the medley relay for girls report
to the clerk of the course."

"That's us," Go said. "Here we go."

Ryn cast one last anxious glance up at the
stands and then followed the other three
around the pool. *And I thought I was scared at
cheerleader tryouts,* she thought. *That was nothing, compared with this!*

The second heat was almost finished. They
looked even faster than the first group. But Go
and Lorrie seemed so calm. Maybe by the time
the swim season was over, Ryn would be able to
walk up to the blocks as though she weren't
facing execution.

The timers were reading their watches and recording the times. Ryn reached up to twist her ponytail, forgetting that her hair was short again. She settled for pulling at the short strands.

"Get wet," the starter called.

Ryn looked at him openmouthed. Go smiled. "That just means we can all dive in and get the feel of the water."

For a few minutes the pool was full of lively bodies. Then the referee blew his whistle, and they climbed back onto the deck. Ryn noticed that Lorrie was signaling GoGo with her eyes.

"What's the matter?" Ryn asked anxiously.

"It's nothing," Go said, trying to brush off her question.

"Go, tell me," Ryn ordered.

"It's just that team in Lane Three, Hollydale," Go said easily. "They've got a pretty good free-styler." Go looked at the pool deck.

Lorrie was staring off into space. Now Marci caught Ryn's concern. "Just how good?" she demanded.

Lorrie and Go exchanged glances. "Tell them," Go said grimly.

Lorrie sighed. "She holds the state record in the fifty-yard freestyle."

Ryn felt her muscles turn to stone. She was

matched against a state champion!

"Backstrokers in the water," the starter called. Hurriedly the four girls clasped hands for luck; then Lorrie climbed down into the pool.

The crowd quieted for the start. "We have to stay behind the timers until the gun goes off," Go whispered.

"All right, ladies," the starter called. "This is the two-hundred-yard medley relay. Each swimmer will swim two lengths—backstroke, breaststroke, butterfly, and any other stroke, in that order." He paused to cock his gun. "Take your mark."

The backstrokers pulled themselves up into a crouch against the blocks. The gun fired, and they arched back and out into the water. Lorrie had a good start. Going across the pool she was moving stroke for stroke with Lanes Three and Four.

They were nearing the wall, and Lorrie went into her flip. It was a good turn. She was out of it and on her way back, ahead of the others.

Marci climbed up on the block, while Go and Ryn clutched at each other's hands. "Go, Lorrie; move it!" GoGo shouted. Ryn tried to shout, too, but her vocal cords were paralyzed.

Lorrie was increasing her lead. She was a good

body-length ahead of the Hollydale swimmer in Lane Three as they came into the wall.

Marci crouched on the block, and, as Lorrie's hand touched the wall, she took off. Ryn held her breath. Marci was good, but as she pulled her way across the pool, the girl in Lane Three was gaining on her. Their narrow lead was dwindling fast. Marci hit the far wall and pushed off hard, but as she came back to the surface, Lane Three was ahead of her.

"Pull, pull, pull!" Go shouted. She gave Ryn's hand a last squeeze for luck, then climbed up on the block.

"Pull, Marci, pull," Ryn breathed. Lane Three was increasing her lead, and now Lane Four was moving up on them.

Hollydale touched up in Lane Three, and their flyer was off. "Hurry, Marci," Lorrie gasped. Marci's last few strokes seemed to take forever, but finally she was at the wall, and GoGo was in the water.

Hollydale had a good four or five yards head start, but GoGo was in rare form. Her strong arms seemed to throw the water away as she arched her way forward. Go was closing the gap, sweeping through the water. She was passing Lane Three, hitting the wall, whipping around.

"Get up there and go, Ryn," Lorrie urged. "You can do it!"

Ryn climbed up on the block, but her legs felt so weak, she didn't know how they could hold her. She looked anxiously across at the Hollydale freestyler waiting on the block in Lane Three. She was as trim and muscular as a boy. *State champ,* Ryn thought tensely. *Just don't make me look too stupid.*

Go was pulling well ahead of the others now. She was going to give Ryn a few yards head start, a fighting chance, anyway.

"Just put your head down and go," Marci urged.

"And don't look around. Just swim," Lorrie shouted. "Come on, GoGo!"

Ryn crouched for the start as Go swooped toward the wall. "Now!" Lorrie yelled.

Ryn flung herself into the water. Her brain had stopped functioning, but her arms and legs were whirling as fast as they could move. *Nancy's drowning,* she told herself. *Got to save Nancy.*

Where was Lane Three? If she could only take the time to turn her head and look around. Her fast turns for breath were too quick for sight-seeing.

But there was the wall. Ryn gulped at the air

and went down into her flip. Her legs whipped
around, and she shoved against the wall with all
her strength, cutting through the water like an
arrow.

Had Three passed her already? If only she
could see some sign of her. There was nothing
to do but keep fighting. *Got to save Nancy, got to
save Nancy,* Ryn thought with each pull of her
arms. The water and the lane markers were just
a blur. *Got to save Nancy.*

She was coming in to the finish. *Mustn't slow
down. Swim right into the wall.* She put on her
last burst of strength, and suddenly her hand was
against the tile.

She clung to the gutter and turned her head
wearily toward Lane Three. The Hollydale
swimmer was just coming into the finish.

"Ryn, you did it!" Go was screaming.

"What a swim!" Lorrie shouted.

They reached down to pull her up onto the
pool deck. "You were great, Ryn." Marci was
dancing with excitement.

"Ryn, she hardly gained on you at all," GoGo
gloated.

"What happened?" Ryn murmured. "I didn't
know what was going on."

"She started out strong, and she seemed to be

gaining on you, but I think that after the turn, she knew she couldn't make it. You held your lead all the way back."

"Whew!" Ryn gasped. "I think I better sit down somewhere."

They had started back around the pool deck, when the loudspeaker blared. "Ladies and gentlemen, congratulations to Coral Cove High. Their time in the medley relay was one and two-tenths seconds under the existing state record."

There was a roar of applause from the crowd. Ryn felt her knees starting to sag. Tom was rushing around the pool to meet them. He gave Go a giant bear hug and then threw an arm around Ryn. "You little rascal," he laughed. "I didn't know you were a fighter like that."

Ryndy grinned. "I've got a mean streak," she confessed.

"Coach is sorry now that he didn't enter you in an individual event, the fifty free, but he was afraid it would scare you off the team in your first meet."

"It would have," Ryn assured him. "I've never been so scared in my life. Besides, without that lead Go gave me, I'd have been trailing the whole pack."

"I doubt that," Tom said, laughing. "You

looked like a supersonic jet."

The team crowded around them now, slapping them on the backs, pumping their hands. Coach was almost bursting. "Ryn, I have to tell you," he said. "I thought we could win it, but I never expected this."

Ryn was overwhelmed by the praise, but there was still one section of the audience she wanted to hear from. "Coach, is it all right if I go up in the stands now? My sister's here from college." She didn't have to mention how much she wanted to see Dirk.

"Ryn, you can have the moon if you want it," Coach announced, his face beaming.

Ryn climbed the wall and slid under the iron railing that separated the spectators from the swimming area. Her family was finally sitting down again in their seats, but Dirk was hurrying down the stairs to meet her.

He didn't seem the least concerned about the fact that they were being observed by her mother, her father, her sister, and several hundred spectators. He lifted her off the ground and kissed her firmly. "You're the greatest, Ryn Drews."

Ryn blushed, but she clung to his arm as they climbed back up the steps to her family. They all hugged her proudly as Dirk tucked her into a seat between him and Val.

Val was bubbling with excitement. "So, we finally have an athlete in the family. Oh, Ryn, you don't know how I envy you. I always wished that I was good enough to make the Coral Cove swim team."

Ryn stared at her in astonishment. Val—envied her?

Ryn turned to look at Dirk. He was nodding with satisfaction. His arm slid around her waist, and the smile in his eyes said, *I told you so.*

Ryn settled back in contentment to watch the rest of the meet. She had wasted a lot of time the past year, she realized, yearning for the wrong things and the wrong people. It was hard to believe now that she had thought her life was over because she couldn't be a cheerleader. It was even harder to realize that she had ever mooned over Brad Hamilton or wept into her pillow because she couldn't be one of her sisters. Being Ryndy Drews was just great, and being Dirk Hudson's girl was even greater.

She looked at Val now, with a glint of mischief in her eye. "Tomorrow I want you to meet my best boyfriend," she announced.

Val looked at her in confusion. "You mean—" She glanced questioningly at Dirk.

"No, his name is Pieter." Ryn smiled. "To-morrow we have a big date to take him home from the hospital."

She felt Dirk's arm tighten around her waist, and she breathed a sigh of pure joy.

Whitman CLASSICS and ANTHOLOGIES

Black Beauty

Little Women

Heidi

Heidi Grows Up

Tom Sawyer

Huckleberry Finn

The Call of the Wild

Treasure Island

Alice in Wonderland

The Wonderful Wizard of Oz

Famous Fairy Tales

Algonquin: The Story of a Great Dog

Tales of Poe

SHORT STORY COLLECTIONS

A Batch of the Best (Stories for Girls)

Like It Is (Stories for Girls)

Shudders

Golden Prize

That's Our Cleo! *(New)*

Way Out *(New)*

Whitman NOVELS FOR GIRLS

Spirit Town

Gypsy From Nowhere

The Family Name

True to You

Practically Twins

Make-Believe Daughter

The Silver Seven

Bicycles North! *(New)*

Whitman ADVENTURE and MYSTERY Books

THE TRIXIE BELDEN SERIES
16 Exciting Titles

MEG MYSTERIES
The Disappearing
Diamonds
The Secret of the
Witch's Stairway
The Treasure Nobody
Saw
The Ghost of Hidden
Springs
The Mystery of the
Black-Magic Cave
Mystery in Williamsburg

DONNA PARKER
Takes a Giant Step
On Her Own
Mystery at Arawak
Special Agent

KIM ALDRICH MYSTERIES
Miscalculated Risk
Silent Partner
The Deep Six *(New)*
The Long Shot *(New)*

TELEVISION FAVORITES
Lassie
Lost in the Snow
Trouble at Panter's
Lake
The Mod Squad
Hawaii Five-O
Family Affair

SPORTS AND ADVENTURE STORIES
Throw the Long Bomb!
(Football)
Basket Fever (Basketball)
Cellar Team (Baseball)
Drag Strip Danger
(Racing)
Divers Down!
(Undersea Adventure)

TEE-BO, THE TALKING DOG
2 Titles in This
Rollicking New Series